How to Disappear Completely

a novel

David Bowick

ISBN 978-0-578-00488-4

Edited by Armond Bagdasarian
Text set in Electra LT

Manufactured in the United States
Wood and Lead Publishing

So much I wrote was impacted deeply by the music that I was listening to and often even included it in the story, so I deemed it appropriate to have a soundtrack from the story. Below is a listing of albums that I listened to when I was writing each particular chapter. I'd recommend checking them all out at some point.

If you have the albums, put them on in the background as you're reading it and it'll be as if you were there as I were writing. Who knows, it might even add a new dimension to the story.

Chapter 1
The Presidents of the United States of America – self-titled

Chapter 2
Danny Elfman - Beetlejuice

Chapter 3
XM Radio - 80s channel
Mayday Parade - A lesson in Romantics

Chapter 4
Trentmøller – The Last Resort

Chapter 5
Sugarland – Enjoy the Ride
Rascal Flatts – Me and My Gang
Lifehouse – Who We Are
Nickel Creek – Why Should The Fire Die?

Chapter 6
A Fine Frenzy – One Cell in the Sea

Chapter 7
Massive Attack – Mezzanine
The Presidents of the United States of America - These Are the Good Times People

Chapter 8

Big Bad Voodoo Daddy - Big Bad Voodoo Daddy

Chapter 10
Jay Clifford – Driving Blind
Jimmy Eat World – Chase This Light
Radiohead – Kid A
Junior Boys – So This Is Goodbye

Chapter 11
Radiohead – Kid A

Chapter 12
Yann Tiersen – Le Fabuleux Destin d'Amélie Poulain
Rachel Loy – Love The Mess
Blindside – Blindside
Imogen Heap – Speak For Yourself

Chapter 13
Sevendust – Home
Sigur Rós – Takk…
The Fratellis – Costello Music

Chapter 14
Alder – Long Way Down

How to Disappear Completely

1

It's amazing how fast you can run when there's a fucking rottweiler chasing you. Few domesticated animals can instill such fear in someone as a rottweiler can. Why anyone would ever want to house such a monster is a mystery to me. They're not lovable, they're not cute and they're not beautiful. They slobber on everything, shit everywhere, and could easily eat the face off a child. Lovely. Sign me up for one. Make that two, actually.

But there I was, running like a mongoose chased by a lion on the dry plains of Namibia. I should probably also mention that the devil dog had only had three good legs, one eye, and a terrible bladder problem. He was spraying everywhere as he ran. His fourth gimp leg wasn't functional—it didn't have a knee joint and was a peg leg dragged along by the three good ones. I always imagined that the other legs had to be resentful of the one bad one. It just coasted along on the energy of the others, not contributing anything, like a child living at home with his parents after college. Yet somehow, by the will of some loving god, he could run. Fast. All I could think about as I ran was how I could first kill the damn thing and make it look like an accident. Run through traffic and hope he gets hit? Feasible, but also likely that I'd be struck by a car, which has never been on my to-do list. I've never even broken a toe. Call me adventurous.

So I did what any respectable, scared 20-something male would do—I turned around, squared my position, looked around to see if there was anyone watching and I kicked the thing smack in the face. It was a spectacular performance. Any soccer player would have agreed that I was blessed in that moment with perfect technique—a divine gift delivered to the steel toe King David of my boot. My foot landed just under the jowls of the beast and raised him head first until he made a flip and landed right on his back. I wish that someone had caught it on video. I'd be an overnight star on YouTube. Who wouldn't want to watch an averagely attractive guy kick a three legged, one eyed dog in the face as it urinates all over itself? The correct answer is no one.

For a moment I started to feel sorry for him. He whimpered in a high-pitched whine and panted so heavily that I thought I pushed his ribs halfway into his throat. But then I saw it—still in his mouth, the reason for this whole ridiculousness, now covered in blood. In a moment of self-confidence after my victory, I rolled up my sleeves, took a deep breath and reached a hand in there. Wrapped around one of those nasty teeth was a ring. Not just any ring—the ring.

Eight days, thirteen hours and ten minutes ago I asked my girl to marry me. The ring that I had carefully picked out for her was now wrapped like a lace bow around a beast's tooth. Anyone would wonder why there was such expensive wrapping on a dirty, slobbery present.

I rotated the ring back and forth trying to jog it loose, hoping that the bastard wouldn't suddenly get a boost of energy and bite my hand off.

I put the slime-and blood-covered six-thousand-dollar ring into my pocket and wondered what to do next. People had started to gather around and I had to have a story to get out of this in the clear. Time to turn on the old charm, I thought. Come on high school drama class, don't fail me now. "Help! Please," I shouted, "this dog was hit by a car. Please, anyone."

"Oh, dear," a rotund older lady said, "can you carry him? My husband's clinic is right down this way a few blocks."

It was time to kick it up a notch.

"Thank you so much ma'am. He's been following me for the last few minutes. I think he likes me, but the poor thing just couldn't keep up." Man, I am such a great liar! "Then he crossed the street with me at just the wrong time, and bam. His three good legs couldn't get him across the street fast enough."

When I smiled just then, I'm pretty sure one of my pearly whites had a sheen glow briefly, like in those old Pepsi commercials. *Enjoy a Pepsi. Ding!*

"Oh, the poor thing. Come on."

I picked up Satan though it took all my remaining energy. I was surprised by my own strength. It's amazing what your body can do after you have triumphed over the Devil himself. His body was limp in my arms and it was difficult to get a good grip on him. After a couple of awkward poses together, we finally settled into a pace that worked for both of us and we stopped stepping on each others toes.

The woman and I commiserated on our short walk to her husband's office. I learned that her name was Darla (are you kidding me?) and her husband was

Herbert. Herbert and Darla Tanis. What year is this and where am I again? They'd been married for 20 years and have many pets. No rottweilers, though, of course. If you pictured a 45-year-old nice fat woman, she fits that image to a 't'. Big eyes, short, stubby arms just long enough to wrap a huge hug around a large child or small man. Dark brown hair and a dated half dress/half muumuu graced her with surprising dignity, much like I've pictured Mother Goose to look. The only other stereotype that I've seen fit someone so perfectly was my Italian roommate in college. Every time he was offered food, he yelled, "L'appetito vien mangiando," as any good Italian does apparently.

We rounded the corner and the Tanis Animal Clinic was a few doors down from there. It was a handsome establishment in the middle of a somewhat dumpy street. I wondered how I had never noticed the clinic before. When we walked in the doors I was transported back to the 50s. I might as well have walked into a soda bar, with girls in beehive, and boys with pompadours. A young couple sipping from a milkshake from a glass with two straws, gazing at each other, wondering when and how they might get to lover's lane for some hanky panky without their parents finding out.

A thick, stately man paraded out from the back who I could only assume was the big man himself. He was balding and pretty short—just big enough for Darla to wrap her arms around, I thought chuckling silently and shaking my head. Herbert was one of the few men that looked right bald. Some bald men you see and think, eeeehhhhh, that's unfortunate, and try your best not to stare. With Herbert, though, it worked. I bet that if he made the exclusive guest list to heaven, he'd still be bald (because, well, it's Herbert Tanis—bald man extraordinaire) and God would parade him around as a trophy of the aging male.

"Goodness!" he exclaimed, as a man of his time would be expected to say in that situation.

"Oh Herby." Ha. *Herby.* "I was bringing you your lunch and I came across these two. Is there anything you can do?"

"He looks pretty bad, but let's see what we can do. Bring him in here."

We followed the trophy through a short hallway lined with photos of happy clients and their mended pets. I took note of how many rottweilers I saw. Precisely zero. The room looked like a typical doctor's office except that it was actually pretty comfortable. It didn't feel like death or sickness, but rather like a blanket of fur that you might snuggle into for a while before realizing that it is, in fact, the carcass of a dead animal and you want it off you immediately.

I laid Hades onto the metal table and he was still bleeding, panting and whimpering. For the first time, I started to feel sorry for the dog as he looked at me in pain. I put my hand into my pocket to finger the ring, making sure it was still there. Herbert took a few diagnostics and asked me questions about what happened, who's dog it was and other background information that I utterly lied about with an air of honesty. I felt like a politician telling his people what they want to hear. Lying is ok when it's good for the system, right?

I told him in detail about how I didn't know who's dog it was and how sad it was the condition he was in, what with its three good legs, one eye and bladder infection. Luckily he had peed all the liquid out of his body when I rapped him and there was none left to squirt around the sterile clinic, but the stench of the urine had stained his fur. He was wearing a tag that identified him, but I said that I didn't know the owner or how he got so far away from home. I recounted my story as best I could. I was a true hero in this epic, stopping to help a poor animal out of my busy schedule because it's what a good person should do. At one point Darla pushed her bottom lip out and pouted with an 'aww' thrown in there.

"Well, this guy's in pretty bad shape here," Herb said. "His jaw is fractured and there's a pulled muscle and some bruising in his neck and hind legs."

"Is there anything we can do?" asked Darla.

"We should try and get ahold of the owner—a Ms. Allison Grayson." He read from the tag. "I'm sure she'll want to know where her dog is and that this kind man may very well have saved his life. There's nothing we can really do for him except give him some pills for the pain and wait for him to heal by himself." The doctor turned to go call the number on the dog's tag.

Interesting twist, I thought: Cold-blooded ninja warrior turned hero. It was a good plan if for no other reason than to make her feel sorry for me. Before the doctor made it out of the door I interrupted: "I'll carry him to her house," I said in a kind tone. "It's not that far from here and it's on my way anyways."

"What a kind man you are." Darla whimpered.

"You sure are, a true samaritan." Echoed Herbert. "Please tell Ms. Grayson that this service is on the house because of your generosity and that if he ever gets sick again that our doors are always open."

"I will tell her and sing your praises," I said with conviction.

He finished cleaning up Satan and gave me a sample bottle of pain pills to give to Allison. Ms. Grayson was not a name I would ever think to call her again. Not after all this bullshit. Who knows though, for a second I thought that things could turn out differently after I bring her poor dog back home from his long, painful, and much deserved experience.

2

I rang the doorbell and waited for a minute. The Antichrist was getting pretty heavy in my arms. I'm not made of much brawn and this 100-pound beast was getting the best of my strength. I felt like Christopher Robin holding Pooh bear up to get some honey, except there was no honey and this creature was not at all cuddly. I considered dropping him on the stoop as a final revenge, but my story would be blown if she opened the door at that moment. So I waited.

I heard footsteps come closer and closer to the door, and then silence. With wooden floors it's hard to hide your movements and someone outside can always tell when you come to the door but don't answer. They can even hear you walk away and know you just don't want to see them. If she decided not to open the door and to walk away it would be like watching her deliberately not answer her cell phone if I called from 20 yards away.

I'm sure she could only see my mug and not her precious beast as she peeked through the eyehole to see who it was. She suddenly swung the door open in a huff as if she were about to scream and slap me across the face–but then she gasped. "Oh my God!" she yelled. "What the hell happened?" The yelling turned to sobs as she began to pet her dog. Well I couldn't very well tell her the truth and I sure wasn't going to tell her why he started to chase me to begin with, so I retold the story as Darla remembered it. Her version was rife with emotional torment, like a made for TV movie. Mine was CNN. Telling the story for the third time was much easier and the facts starting to feel like truth to me, and thus they would to everyone else.

She invited me in and I laid Satan onto the sofa. Allison stroked his head as I recounted every false detail. She was eating up every word like fine soft cheese, savoring each bite. I was a true wordsmith pulling out words I didn't know I knew and metaphors even Billy Collins would approve of. I told her all about Darla and Herbert who was the 'true' hero in this story. I had to fight myself not to wink and give a thumbs up as I said it. When I got to the part where I carried the dog home, she threw her arms around me and showered me in thank yous.

Unsure of what to do next, I said I was in a hurry and just wanted to make sure she heard what happened. I gave her the pills, repeated the dosage info Herbert had told me, and stood up. I looked at the dog and couldn't tell whether he was looking at me as an enemy or his saviour. Technically I was both, as most heroes are, but dogs don't remember all that much anyways, right? If they could talk, then there might be some issues, but as far as science knows right now, they can't and I was safe.

She started to baby talk the devil dog as I opened the door to leave. God I hate baby-talking to animals, especially to fucking rottweilers. They're animals not children. I'm not saying we shouldn't be nice to animals, but don't treat them like children. That's just sad.

On the walk home that afternoon, I couldn't quite decide whether I felt exhilarated by my performances or depressed about everything that happened before the debacle.

The morning before, I had woken up hopeful about myself with Allison. I had bought a ring that cost me six months worth of work and had planned the perfect proposal.

A friend of mine's dad owned a traveling carnival. I told him my elaborate plan and convinced him to keep the carnival open an extra night so that we could have our own private party. All he'd asked in return was that I try and convince his son Greg to get his life together. Knowing full well it would never work, I had agreed to try. Greg was one of those guys who didn't really have any goals. He lived the life of a typical fraternity jock even though he was neither a jock nor in a fraternity.

Later that day, when we got to the carnival, Allison had no idea that I had set everything up just for us. I guess she thought that it was just an unusually slow night because she didn't seem to find it strange that we were the only ones there.

Eventually, after wasting some money trying to win her god-awful stuffed animals that she'd throw away in a week or so, I got us onto the Ferris wheel and asked the lovely hostess to let us hang out at the top for a while. It's amazing what a $20 bill will get you from a carnie. I could have gotten her to cluck like a chicken, but decided that wasn't all that romantic. It's too bad she wasn't a violinist, a poet, or something else that would be useful on a romantic evening. As we sat there at the top of the wheel looking out over the Boston skyline across the Charles, I doused her with a bucket of words, in my best lover's tone. I pulled out some "Remember when we..." moments which girls always melt for. As she was dripping into a puddle, I pulled out the ring and said the words that every man loves to dread.

Despite a slight hesitation, her answer started out perfect with an "Oh, Josh." The ring had one of those lights inside the case that made it shimmer like a star and it really did look beautiful (six grand's worth). Then came the worst words that can be said after a proposal. "Can we talk about this?"

Are you fucking kidding me?

"It's just that I don't know if I'm ready for that yet."

Are you fucking kidding me?

"You know I love you so much."

I briefly debated jumping off and wondered how long it would take until I finally hit the ground. Instead, I yelled down to the carnie to bring us down.

"Josh."

Are you fucking kidding me?

"Josh. Will you talk to me?"

The only thing I could muster up to say was "I want a corn dog."

When we finally got off the wheel of shame (as I call them now), I marched over to the food vendor area. Unfortunately food was not part of the deal with the owner. Only the rides and a few of the games were open to us. Are you fucking kidding me? I just wanted a goddamn corn dog.

We went back to her place because she wanted to talk, which really meant that she wanted to talk and wanted me to just sit there and not say anything, feigning interest in what she had to say. As we walked in, Satan glared at me and growled. Other than the fact that I hated him in return, I couldn't figure out why he hated me so much. I had never hit him or anything. I had fed him when I was asked to and walked him a few times, though he just tried to escape my grasp the whole time, probably with the urge to eat some defenseless children. We scooted past him as he stared me down the whole way up the stairs to her bedroom. What was once a nest of young love now looked like a battlefield as we both strapped on our armor and got into position.

After a war of ideas on how to get out of this horrible mess, I somehow fell asleep exhausted from battle. She probably kept talking at least 20 minutes after I dozed off. I had a dream that night where carnies were dancing in a circle around the ring chanting in an ancient carnie language the songs of their ancestors. It was oddly entertaining, though disturbing. I half expected Hannibal Lecter to come out and start eating their cold, clammy brains with a nice glass of Chianti before putting on a Bach record and air conducting along. All of a sudden, a rogue carnie drove one of the trucks top speed right into the middle of the campfire. The damage was devastating. I heard the screaming of the ones not killed on impact, but injured severely. The animals' cages had all broken loose and all the lions, tigers, elephants, and other large animals started running around in no particular direction. Eventually the scene quieted down after the sound of the ambulances faded along the dirt road heading back to the city.

When I woke up she had left for work early and left me a note saying that she was glad we talked and that she'd be home for lunch if I was still around. I made it a point to remember not be at lunch with her that afternoon. Besides, I had to go to work.

I worked as Barista at the local Starbucks, churning out over-priced water and bean-based beverages for people who thought they were more important than they really were. Extra hot, double half-caf, non-fat, no-whip Mocha with soy milk. I used to always just think to myself, "Just order the regular one fatty, it's clearly not making a difference." But then again, I needed the job so I just smiled and handed over the drinks hoping that they'd spill it all over themselves and burn some of that loose skin off. Whatever, you've all thought it before too, so don't judge me. Some people just ask for it and I duly give it.

That was my endless routine for 6 hours a day, 6 days a week. It could have been worse, but not by much. Most of the time I just got into a zone and didn't see, feel, or have any real interaction outside of my own mind. It was like when you're driving and 50 miles down the road you suddenly can't remember driving that distance because you were in a trance conjured by the endless stream of white lines ticking like the seconds on a clock rolled out flat.

My goal was to get better at repeating this trance-like state. I wanted to see if I could learn to control it. That'd be a pretty good skill and I could use it daily. The whole day before it would have been a godsend. Especially after all of that proposal mess, I wanted the ability to help me not think of the harsh rejection. So for the rest of the day I decided to practice. I would zone out and make lattés. I became less and less like an employee and more like a robot. No extras, just work. I was super efficient and everything was going well until one lady ordered her usual "Extra hot, double half-caf, non-fat, no-whip Mocha with soy milk."

She stomped through the doors wearing her power suit that was about to bust at the seams from a bunch of powerless and angry cloth. Her sunglasses never came off as she got in line in a huff because she had to wait. She spoke quickly and loudly into her Bluetooth headset talking to someone who probably cared as little about what she was saying as everyone else in the store. I noticed a few other customers roll their eyes at the ridiculousness of her and how typical and contrived her performance was.

Melinda, who works the registers, and I normally worked the same shifts. She was what she was and not much more. I couldn't have cared less about her and rarely spoke to her about anything. On that day, though, she forgot to write soy on the cup and the lady was furious. The fat bitch took a sip of her drink, reeled back, and spit it out, landing a spray of coffee bullets all over me as if I were a paper target in a shooting range. "This is NOT soy milk!" she screamed and proceeded to dry heave a la Jim Carrey in Dumb & Dumber except here it was not at all funny, just sad.

She threw her drink down onto the ground, spilling her Extra hot, double half-caf, non-fat, no-whip Mocha with skim milk all over the floor as well as a few customers who were just minding their own business. I had never seen such a scene. She stood there screaming like an under-qualified military officer who just got promoted because her daddy was an elite officer. She was struggling for command of her soldiers, but everyone knew she didn't deserve any sort of respect and they all just wanted her to shut up.

My boss came out to try and console her, but she wasn't having any of it. Other customers were upset because they were either covered in her coffee or because they now had to wait as all the employees were scrambling to help and clean up.

I looked over at Melinda, dripping in a mix of slobber, espresso and sugar, and then looked down at my shirt. Looking back up to Melinda, she gave me a face that said 'What?' Eventually our boss had to give the lady a bunch of free drink coupons to get her to shut up and leave. It's amazing what you can get in life if you're evil and cause enough trouble. People will just reward your indecencies to try and keep the peace. All the regular people just going along should be rewarded for being regular. All the bitches like her should be clubbed over the head and tossed to the gutter. If it weren't for that whole "justice and law system" thing, then I may very well have gone Fight Club on her.

Marcus, the owner, walked over to us shaking his head. "Alright you two, will someone tell me what the hell that was all about?"

"The cup didn't say soy." I said politely.

"What? It sure did. He just didn't read it right." Melinda retorted.

Marcus looked at the two of us and went to go find the cup that had caused the whole mess. He picked it up, wiped it off and came back over. By now, all the coffee had erased or smeared most of what Melinda wrote. There was really no telling what was there originally.

"Look. I understand that she's just exceptionally nuts and completely out of her tree, but we can't have people do that in our store, so we have to make sure their orders are right. OK? Please don't let this happen again. Either of you."

Melinda and I agreed to be more aware and Marcus retreated to the office in the back. I grabbed a napkin to try and dry some of the gunk off of me, but it would have taken more napkins than the store had to get me clean. So I decided to be disgusting the rest of the day and proudly display my wounds from that battle.

I debated whether or not to drift off into a trance again but after you've been through something like that, it makes you care even less. I was contemplating revenge on Melinda when I heard a "Whoa, what happened to you?" I looked up and saw the last person in the world that I wanted to see. Allison. I would have rather had the Extra hot, double half-caf, non-fat, no-whip Mocha with soy milk lady come back and spit in my face again than to see her.

"Look, I really don't want to talk about it."

"Alrighty, well I didn't see you at lunch today so I thought I'd see if you were here."

"Well here I am."

"You want to come over after work?"

"After a day like this I don't really think I'll be in a great mood." Not to mention a night like last night.

"Oh. Ok. Well if you change your mind, I'll be there just hanging out, ok?"

"Yeah, ok." There's no way in hell that's going to happen.

She looked almost as defeated as Marcus did a few minutes ago and I couldn't help but smile a little bit inside for my small win. It's amazing that after shooting you in the heart, girls will often want to smile and cuddle afterwards. What they don't realize is that most of the time we just want to get them back. We want revenge. Not serious revenge, just little victories here and there. She retreated and rounded the corner outside the store then faded away.

It wasn't until two showers later that I felt like I got myself clean from the fat bitch spittle. I still shudder thinking about it. The next day, she came back. That Extra hot, double half-caf, non-fat, no-whip Mocha with soy milk lady and her stupid face. I saw her walk in and was tempted to make whatever it was wrong on purpose just to see what would happen. I looked over and Melinda's face hardened as soon as she saw the woman.

Of course she used one of her many free drink coupons and walked briskly to wait for her cup, standing in front of everyone who was already waiting patiently. "Let's go, I'm in a hurry," she said, just begging me to forego my generally high sense of morality. "Come on!" she yelled again. "And could you maybe try and make it right this time?"

"Coming right up." I said cheerfully. After giving the other satisfied customers their drinks I finally started making hers. My mind was racing trying to think of what I could do and suddenly it hit me. The adrenaline took me by the hand and helped me as I took her Extra hot, double half-caf, non-fat, no-whip Mocha with soy milk, put the lid on loosely and 'tripped' as I took a small step over to give it to her. The cup flew out of my hands and my God was it beautiful. I wish the Planet Earth video crew were there to film it at 100 frames per second so that we could watch it again at super slow motion in all of it's glory.

The lid that was loosely placed on the cup came off first as the first bits of coffee flew out. The cup got some good air as it left my hands and I had just enough time to see a reaction before the bomb landed. Her face was pure joy to my eyes. Just as her mouth started to open up into a scream, her Extra hot, double half-caf, non-fat, no-whip Mocha with soy milk landed on her face first, then her chest and the last little bits made it all the way to her feet. Like a cartoon, the cup hit her square on the head a hair later than the coffee did. I was an unbelievable shot. Everywhere that it landed it slid downward, around all her fatty rolls, invading every crevice and planting flags at each stop to claim its territory. The bloodcurdling scream she belched resounded so loudly that a few other people dropped their own drinks on the floor in surprise.

The new guy, eager to be helpful, rushed over to the woman with a whole ream of napkins to help get her dry. Marcus ran out of the back and as he saw the whale, he ran full speed over to her almost knocking over the display of Starbucks sponsored CDs and a few customers as well. After assessing the situation, looking at the woman and then Melinda, he looked straight at me. I had never seen that look in anyone before. He looked the way Jack the Ripper must have just before he carried out his well-planned murders. I tried to act surprised, but I was enjoying the moment too much to pull it off with any sort of conviction, and he saw my game. "Josh. My office. Now! Oh, God, you have got to be kidding me."

I slowly and triumphantly removed my apron and in my head I heard everyone in the place erupt into applause. I'm sure a few people who were there had seen what happened before and had seen her in the store a few other times as well. I hoped that someone understood and smiled with a nod while seeing the whole thing play out. Melinda looked at me as if she had just gotten smacked across the face by her best friend without provocation. Slightly bowing every few steps along the way, I brushed past Melinda, pushed open the door and arrived backstage to my green room.

It didn't occur to me until a few minutes later that this would end up hurting me pretty bad. I was still running on the fumes of my high to care much, but it all came to a screeching halt when Marcus came back in looking like Wile E. Coyote with the Road Runner in his sight.

3

Marcus beat my ear for an hour or so until he finally collapsed like a lover after a marathon romp in the sack. As big of a man as he was, he had a surprisingly small angry tone. Normally in the equation of men, the size of the man is directly proportional to the size of his voice capacity. This was not the case with Marcus and it was the sole reason that I didn't fear for my life during his rant. For most of his spiel I drifted in and out of a daydream where I was floating around above Coney Island invisibly as if I were haunting the place. It's odd though, because I've never been to or even seen the island. That's the fun with dreams, they'll lie right back to you.

Needless to say I was let go. I would have fired me on the spot as well, but would have probably tossed in a nice brisk slap across the face or kick in the shins as a severance package. I couldn't really complain as I clearly did it all on purpose. The trick was just going to be finding my next job. Marcus, still exhausted from his tirade, looked as though he needed a cigarette. "Well, do you have anything else to say?" he asked plainly.

"Not really. Frankly, I think it was worth it. She was just the worst."

Marcus had cooled down and now chuckled with me. "Well, at least you've got a good sense of humor."

"Yeah, maybe now I'll open up my own Starbucks across the street. You know I'd get more business."

"You go ahead and try."

I walked out of the office with an odd tranquility surfing along my veins. I laughed out loud as I recounted the last 24 hours. "I'm like a bad movie," I mumbled to a stranger as he walked past me in the opposite direction. Maybe it'll end up being one of those movies that's so bad that it's good, I thought. I thought about going to Allison's, but decided to just forget about her for the night and walked a few more blocks, around the corner and into Our House, a local bar.

The place was pretty dead. After all it was only 5 o'clock. The happy hour crowd was just starting to trickle in with their pea coats and Bluetooth headsets and the jukebox hadn't yet been turned up to eleven. After picking my seat at the bar, I ordered a Jack Daniels on the rocks. The bartender was this guy I'd seen there before, I don't know his name, but the thing about him that stood out is that he always wore the same shirt. Granted I didn't go there all that often, but every time I did he was wearing the same cowboy shirt with blue and brown stripes and mother of pearl buttons. The kicker was this bolo he wore with an Arizona style cattle skull and turquoise stones for eyes.

I downed my first drink in about one and a half sips and signaled for more by tapping on the rim. Bolo came over and poured me another drink. I looked up at the TV and the news happened to be on. I always hated the news. It's always the same and we never actually learn anything. Someone died, a new medical study says we can't eat something that we all eat regularly, another pharmaceutical bought their way into a piece about how their drug is the new best thing, more killing, etc. (The only thing I'd steal from our Canadian brothers to the north is their news. They actually have news that matters.) They were doing a piece that night on the carnival that had been in town. Apparently one of their employees had been drinking and rammed one of their trucks into the camp killing 12 and injuring 9.

The camera zoomed in on the smoldering campfire with branches of metal and debris around it. Broken cages, aimless animals, corn dogs and cotton candy were strewn about mingled with all the orphaned stuffed animals keeping them company. I couldn't really grasp right away what I was seeing on the screen. It all seemed very familiar though I couldn't figure out why. I must have had my mouth hanging or something because Bolo asked me, "Hey, you alright?"

"Yeah, I just...I was just there the other night."

"Oh the carnival, huh. That's some shit, right? I wonder what made him do it."

"You think he did it on purpose?"

"That's what they're saying. Either that or he's just got really bad aim."

"I proposed to my girl there last night."

"Oh congratulations."

"She didn't say yes."

"Oh."

"..."

"Here, this one's on me."

"Thanks."

We bantered a bit as the place started to fill up. The bar always drew a strangely eclectic crowd. Of course the local college kids came in with their fake IDs and were normally accepted without question. There were often businessmen, because of the college girls; older gay women, because of the college girls; blue-collar types, because of the college girls, and then the other 20-30 somethings as well. It's amazing the demand for college girls. Try to work on a girl 5 years older and you're ten times more likely to actually get somewhere with her, flattered that you passed up all the newer, younger models.

The pool table lit up with its constellation of balls—new solar systems being created every ten minutes or so. It was an amazing universe. I sometimes felt like God watching it all happen from the outside. Right as I was admiring a constellation that looked like a smiley face, a soft voice bubbled, "Hey, can I sit here?"

"Um...sure, yeah." I stammered.

"It's my birthday!"

"Happy Birthday."

"Are you going to buy me a drink or what?"

"Oh, um, yeah. What's your drink?"

"I don't know, something fun."

I waved Bolo over.

"So, it's her birthday and she wants something fun."

"How about a couple buttery nipples."

"Ha! What's that?" She giggled. I couldn't help but cringe a little at that giggle.

"Warm butterscotch schnapps. It's pretty amazing." Bolo replied.

"Make two," I said. "Aren't you here with anyone else?"

"Yeah, my friends are over there."

"Are you sure you don't want them to drink with you?"

"No, that's why I came over here."

"Oh, ok. Two it is barkeep."

Bolo twirled the schnapps bottle around his finger like a cowboy in a shootout at high noon and poured two shots, then returned the bottle to its holster and pushed the drinks over to us.

"How about a toast?" She smiled.

"Sure. Let's see," God I'm awful at toasts.

"Make it good, it's my birthday."

I sighed, closed my eyes, took a deep breath and said, "Ok here we go. Wait, what's your name?"

"I thought you would never ask." She leaned in so close to my ear that I could feel her lips brush my ear as she spoke, "Nicole."

I stayed there a second savoring that feeling, then snapped back to reality.

"To Nicole. May her birthday be as full of life as the stars in her eyes." I said. Where did that come from?

For a moment she didn't say anything. She just looked at me with a touch of sadness that I felt drip to my feet as if I just stepped into a light rain. The moment passed and she screamed, "WHOOOO!"

We both took our shots and I felt the warmth coat the lining of my throat and fade slowly down into my stomach. "My name is Josh." I said.

"Well, let's have another, Josh." Nicole said with a slight hint of rebellion. I will rebel against the world by drinking butterscotch schnapps, I thought. If only Stalin had access to butterscotch schnapps instead of Vodka, he may not have been such a dick.

Bolo poured us another and without a word we downed our second.

"One more?" I tossed the words out into the booze filled haze unsure of why.

"Yes." Her neck started to loosen up. You're already tipsy? I thought to myself. I've been here drinking whiskey for a few hours already. She sat on the edge of her barstool like a child waiting to open her first present at a birthday party. Bolo poured us another two short glasses. Mid-shot, she exclaimed as loud as she could with a mouth full of schnapps. "Mm Mm!"

She slammed her glass down onto the bar and jumped up to her feet. "This is my song," she screamed as she bobbed her head back and forth. The whole night they'd been doing an 80s theme with the tunes. *Take on me. Take on me. Take me up.* "Let's go dance." As any guy would do, I tried to keep us at the bar and as far away from the dance floor as possible. She was surprisingly strong, though, and pulled me up out of my seat. She bounced with the beat all the way over to a small open area and kept bouncing full force, occasionally doing that Flashdance running in place move.

I realized then that I hadn't been off the barstool since I had gotten there at 5 and was more drunk than I realized. The dangling Christmas lights mixed in with the neon beer signs and danced together with the beat. I looked over to Nicole, who was clearly in her own world, uncaring of everyone around her and I couldn't help but feel a bit jealous of being so care free. After a second, I let the alcohol finally take the wheel in my head and I started moving. "Yay!" she exclaimed as I bounced my legs. After the alcohol got used to controlling the movement of the legs, my arms started swirling about. Piece by piece, I was letting go of my body parts, succumbing to the capable but awkward force of the sauce.

Song after song we danced. It was something I had never done before and something that she was clearly an expert at. Eventually, after some more 80s classics of Genesis, Tears for Fears, Frankie Goes to Hollywood, Paula Abdul, Gloria Estefan, Journey, and Modern English, my bladder was screaming for my attention like a child that wouldn't be ignored. "I'll be right back." I tried to say over the music.

"Ok." She replied melodically in sync with the music.

The room slid slowly back and forth as I walked as if I were on a large boat floating on the sea. Arrghh, I thought as I pushed open the door to the bathroom with a hooked index finger. Public restrooms are one of my least favorite places. Surrounded by men with their pants down and their dicks hanging out like a shady porn theatre with sticky floors. That's the image that always comes in my head as I wedge myself into a tightly packed line of urinals.

After a shake or two and a shiver that ran briskly down my spine, I washed my hands and left the theater. I made my way past the businessmen, college girls, and the rockstar wannabes back to where Nicole was dancing. I paused a moment, made sure I was is in the right spot, furrowed my eyebrows and started looking around. I stood on my tippy-toes trying to get a better view but couldn't find her anywhere. I walked back over to Bolo and asked, "Hey have you seen the Buttery Nipples girl?"

"I don't hear that nearly often enough," he smirked hoping for some recognition or return joke. He noticed my lack of interest and finally said "I haven't seen her since you guys went over to dance. Sweet moves by the way."

"Thanks." I paid my tab, ran outside past the bouncer who was surprisingly small and looked around hoping to see her somewhere. Twenty minutes ago I could have cared less about this girl, but somewhere between A-Ha and Fleetwood Mac something happened. I walked around the block once just for good measure before giving up completely. I walked home that night trying to make sense of my life. I'd always known the epithet 'when it rains it pours', but it rarely rained over me. It felt as if I was suddenly walking around in wet socks, weighing my feet down as if two kids were sitting on my feet with their legs wrapped around mine.

At least I could walk. The wonder of Boston, as a 20-something, is that you don't have to drive anywhere and probably wouldn't even if you could afford it. Drink and drink and then just walk home. My feet slowly started to lighten up as I started to let everything go bit by bit. I ran up the stoop to my apartment, opened the door and fell face down onto my bed. It's amazing how a bed feels more like a home than any other part of a house.

That night I dreamt of Nicole. Her hair the color of a Strawberry-banana smoothie, her eyes the dark blue/grey of ocean horizon after it rains over the sea. It's amazing how fast it can happen. Infatuation should be prescribed as a drug for the sullen or depressed. What a job that would be, to be the object of affection for the troubled. It's one of the few feelings that instantly makes everything else in the world seem trivial. Love doesn't even quite compare. There are so many degrees of love that sometimes it's just there in the background like a jazz guitar player riffing standards in the back of your mind. Sometimes you notice him as he plucks out a tune you actually recognize, but the rest of the time he's just kind of there.

In my dream I saw her walking down Massachusetts Avenue toward Cambridge. She was smoking an Ultra Light and bobbing her head to the sounds of her iPod. The dream zoomed in closer to her and I could hear her listening to what was probably her favorite Mayday Parade song—*I had a dream last night we drove out to see Las Vegas. We lost ourselves in the bright lights, I wish you could have seen us.* I couldn't have imagined anything else for her to listen to—just obscure enough to be cool, but well known enough for others to know how cool.

I just floated above her for a while and watched her, trying to figure her out. There is no greater mystery than a love interest when you first meet them—so much to learn and so many unknowns. What's her favorite food? What's she into? All the things that would eventually be made known in a relationship. (I knew everything there was to know about Allison, and though there's certainly something great about that, I realized that I missed the mystery.) I followed her all the way over to the MIT campus before I woke up to my bladder elbowing my insides reminding me I had to go. I was still in my clothes from last night and most likely in the position that I had fallen into when I first got home. Now that's sleeping, I thought.

A quick flush and I plopped back down into bed. Reaching over to my nightstand, I looked at my cell phone and saw that Allison had called a few times the night before. I played the message back on speakerphone as I rolled out of bed again to brush my teeth. "Hey Josh, it's Allison. Hey I just was wondering if maybe we could talk some more. I feel like things have been left on a weird note and I was hoping that we could work things out. Give me a call when you get a chance. Bye."

So much has happened since I saw you last, I thought. Less than 24 hours ago I had a job and wasn't hopelessly infatuated with another girl that I didn't know if I'll ever see again. I'm a different person entirely. A brief look outside told me that it was going to be a nice day and dammit I was going to enjoy it while I could. I put on some clothes, grabbed my bag, some tunes, a book and walked out the door.

4

When you have no specific goals for a day, it's amazing what you can come up with to do. I'd been so conditioned to the routines of work and life with Allison, that being free of both of those things (Allison pending) was kind of like a snow day. I felt like I could do anything and was probably going to try. I decided to take a leisurely walk down Newbury Street, something I hadn't done in a long time because Allison hated it. I thought about what else I could do now without Allison dictating our agendas as I passed by my favorite local homeless man. Just before rounding the corner, I walked past Sweet & Nasty, a specialty adult toy and cake shoppe. That place always gets me—I should work there, I thought as I turned onto Newbury. I popped into Newbury Comics to check out some new records. After you haven't been in a record store for a while (because you buy all your music on iTunes), you suddenly remember why record stores are so great. Everyone is there for one purpose: the music. Whatever your musical tastes are you can find something that you'll like and most likely someone else there who likes the same thing, no matter how bizarre it may be.

The line at JP Licks had died down a bit after I left Newbury Comics with nothing but a slight contact high, so I moseyed on in and got an ice cream cone. The guy at the counter kept looking at me, clearly thinking that I was cute and that maybe I'd be interested in him, but hey, it's Boston and I was pretty used to it by then. I loved to toy with gay men. I'd speak very clearly in a straight tone, but would occasionally drop in mumbles of obscenities, just quiet enough that it wouldn't be understood. "Here's your change."

I browsed my iPod for the perfect soundtrack to this walk. Scrolling past the classic life-soundtrack tunes of Radiohead, Sigur Rós and Yann Tiersen, I felt like I needed something a bit more obscure. Ah, there it was, Trentmøller. Nothing like some weird electronica to add a mood to life. You know how sometimes when you find the perfect soundtrack to life, you actually feel like you're watching it instead of living it? That's exactly what it felt like as I paraded down the street. I disappeared and in my place was my understudy, and an HD camera with a soap opera filter on to make it all feel even more ethereal. I just sat back with some popcorn and watched as life around me buzzed with caffeine and lust.

This street was amazing, how could anyone not appreciate it? It had everything. The chic flares of expensive grub, hipster shops, bums chanting for change, $20 parking, art galleries, Skate shops, Asian markets, you name it, it was there. It was always good people-watching as well. All the girls who wished they were high fashion broke out their D&G garb and kicked it with their huge sunglasses and tried to look like someone famous.

Eventually I made it down to the Commons and browsed around the local Frisbee players and hippies, who are usually the same, but not in this town. I sat for a while and let my camera-self pan across the landscape, immortalizing each Frisbee toss and kiss for posterity. The spring in Boston was unlike anywhere else. There was a certain magic in the air. After taking in all the scenes that I could, I headed back up towards Newbury to check out the other side of the street.

When I finally made it back to Mass Ave I stopped and looked around, wondering where to now? I turned right and headed back towards my apartment. Instead of going home, though, I kept going until I hit the Charles River and the Longfellow Bridge. About halfway down the bridge, on the other side of the street I saw a girl walking with strawberry blonde hair, bobbing her head as she walked. I squinted a bit to try and get a better look, but I knew it was her. I didn't have enough time to see her face as she passed me going the opposite direction. I couldn't believe it, it had to be her. A second later I had a déja vu to end all déja vu. The feeling hit me so hard I stopped for a moment, almost saying 'ow.' I disregarded all traffic that may have been coming and ran across the street. I was about 20 feet from her. She was wearing those tight jeans with no back pockets. God bless the person who invented the back pocket-less jeans.

I toyed with the idea of catching up to her and tapping her on the shoulder, but we were halfway across the bridge and she probably would have either maced me in the face or kicked me in the groin. Either way I would have most likely fallen over the edge into the freezing Charles to a slow, frigid death. That was out of the question, so I just stayed behind her a bit trying to think of what the chances were that it was actually her. It had to be an absurd a million to one chance. There were 590,763 people in Boston and the area of the city was 89.6 square miles. The chances were too small, I thought, but it has to be her. We finally cleared the 2164.8 feet of the bridge and she turned left and across the street toward the Esplanade.

Again I was struck by a déja vu so hard it broke my stride.

I started to wonder how I could approach her without being creepy or having to say that I'd been following her for about half a mile. I decided to alter my route and walk away from her a bit hoping she'd stop somewhere. About a quarter of a mile down, she sat on a bench looking out over the Charles, right as the song I was listening to came to a final pause. It felt as if time stopped for a second. I couldn't just walk up to her now, I had to either wait a while or walk right in front of her and have her see me. I surveyed the situation to formulate a plan.

There was a small dock leading out over the river right by her bench. Perfect, I said to myself moved forward. Keeping my head down as I walked, I slowly walked past her and got aboard the dock. It seemed more like a raft that was attached by a single rope to the brush than a dock, but I had a plan. I sat down and peered out over the Charles. The college crew teams were practicing their ancient exercises. I wondered how the coxswain was chosen. He didn't have to do anything but yell at everyone else to do the hard work of rowing. How does someone get that gig?

I looked left with my peripheral vision to see her out of the corner of my eye. She was still there, curled up with a book, reading intently. I wondered if she had seen me, or if she would have cared if she had seen me. I have to at least talk to her, I thought. I grabbed my bag and prepared myself as best I could. I'm certainly not an outgoing person and I was even less so with my confidence nearly at empty.

I took a big breath, stood up and looked around. Still there? I began walking back toward the sidewalks and tried to think of something to say. Closer. Closer. Stop. I squeezed my face into my best inquisitive look and said "Nicole?"

Startled, she looked up. "Oh, hey."

"What are the chances, right?"

"Yeah."

I had never felt silence as awkward as this. The air was suddenly tinged with a strange feeling, clinging to every breath I took. I almost choked on it.

"So what happened last night? I came out of the bathroom and you had left."

"Oh, yeah, well I just had to leave. Sorry. I didn't think you'd mind anyway."

I was choking on the heavy air, the words getting harder and harder to get out.

"Actually I was having a great time."

"Really?"

"Yeah, I mean you got me to dance, right? Who else could have done that?" I did a few moves with my arms to jog her memory.

Finally a smile.

"Look, I'm really not very good with guys, you know? I just got out of this bad relationship and I'm just not sure I want to do that again just yet."

"I certainly understand that. I don't really want to get into anything big either. I just asked my girl to marry me two days ago and she said no."

"Ouch."

"You're telling me."

She looked at me for a moment. I could tell she was sizing me up: Was this guy worth continuing a conversation with? "You want to sit down?" she finally said, tentatively.

"Yeah, that'd be great."

We sat on that bench for a while talking about the things you do when you first meet someone. I told her all about my struggles with Allison, the ring, her stupid dog, the carnival proposal, and my recently lost job. I could tell she was judging me a bit about the fact that I had no real career. "So then what do you really want to do?"

"I'm not really sure yet."

"Don't you think you should think about it, especially now that you lost your job?"

She had a good point. "Yeah, you're right."

"Well what do you like to do?"

"I like music, writing, and walking around."

"What do you write?"

"Mostly just little stories, but I try to write a lot of different things."

"What about music reviews?"

"I've never thought of that. I guess it would make sense, but I wouldn't know where to start."

"Well, you should figure that out." She smiled with the same expression that I remembered so fondly from the night before.

After our short analysis of my life, I found out she attended MIT and was studying biological engineering. She tried telling me about what that actually meant, but I got lost before we got very far and made a note to myself to look it up. She was in her 3rd year of school and was trying to plan what she may want to do afterwards. I had never met anyone like her before. She was so completely different than everyone else in my life that I was a little nervous. It felt disorienting, the way it feels when you wake up and it takes a second to realize where you are. She told me all about the relationship she was just in and how it affected her.

She had recently gotten out of a relationship that was very taxing on her life. "He never hit me," she explained, "but I actually lived in fear that he might. For a while I was too scared to even break up with him." She went on a bit more before she stopped suddenly and asked to change the subject. I obliged, feeling weak from just listening to her story.

We chatted for a while and then she said that she had to go to class. "I'll walk you back up to the bridge," I said, trying to be a gentleman. On our short walk we made plans to meet up later that night for dinner at the approachably stylish Redline, at 7. Right before we made it to the bridge, she asked, "Why did you wait so long to talk to me after you saw me?" I was dumbfounded. "I saw you and knew you were following me from the moment you ran across the street."

"Oh I just...I'm not very confident sometimes. I didn't want you to think I was following you."

"But you were." She smiled a devilish grin and looked up at me as a strand of her hair tickled her eyelashes before she slowly brushed it away and back behind her ear.

5

When Nicole left, I just stood there watching her walk away for a moment. Nothing creepy, just watching her go. I was trying to take in as much of her as possible before she was gone, even though I knew that I was going to see her again that night. When she was finally out of sight, I turned the other way and started walking home. Basking in her glow, I made it halfway to my apartment before I had a thought that didn't involve her.

I realized then that I had dreamt about her the night before and saw her walk across that bridge just as she did. I made a note to remind myself to ask her what she was listening to. If it was Mayday Parade, I was going to lose it. I hadn't actively thought to walk that way either. I just did it as if my dream slid into my conscious mind and nudged a few synapses to fire and get my feet moving in the right direction. Then I remembered the dream I had about the carnie massacre and got so creeped out that I stopped walking and some guy ran into the back of me saying "Hey watch it asshole." If we had been driving, he would have gotten the ticket for following too closely, but somehow I was the asshole here.

I'm not really a huge believer in the paranormal or premonitions or anything like that, but two very detailed dreams ended up coming true and it was enough for me to start to believe, or at least to think about believing, that something unusual was going on here. I decided to make a few more stops before I made my way home, to kill some time. I desperately needed some food and decided to get something new to wear for that night. Eventually I made it home and ran up my stoop while trying to get my mind back on Nicole. I threw my stuff down and plopped into bed. I looked at the clock for some reassurance, but only realized how long I had before dinner. Ugh.

I just sat there twiddling my thumbs on the Internet by checking all my accounts. It always amazed me how many passwords I had to remember to find out if people wanted to talk to me. Myspace, Facebook, my 3 email addresses, IM. Toss in the lesser used ones like Netflix, Bank of America, anything to do with bills and it's a wonder we can remember anything else but usernames and passwords. Logging into all of those sites, I got the ever-pleasing result of no messages. None. Not even from Allison. Oh right. Allison. Suddenly it hit me. What the hell was I doing? I was still seeing Allison. Really I haven't done anything wrong, I thought. I wasn't totally sure that tonight was a date, though it sure felt like it was going to be one. Where is the line? Is going out to dinner cheating? I decided that later I should drop by Allison's after she got home from work to finally talk to her about things and see what we could come up with. I had put it off long enough and now at least I didn't feel quite so terrible about her rejection. I realized that I could, and possibly already had, move on.

The day had taken a toll on my body, so I decided I needed a shower. As I took my clothes off, I felt oddly insecure as if someone were watching me from somewhere. It was a feeling I hadn't felt since far before I met Allison and I was curious why it had found its way back to me. I stepped in the shower and just stood there while a barrage of little watery fists pummeled my face, letting them have a go at beating all the bad out of me, letting it wash off my skin and down the drain. Let the rats chew on my problems, I thought.

The cleansing power that the shower provided me was always stronger than any priest or reconciliation would ever provide. The worst part of a shower, of course, was the getting out. Leaving that warm womb of watery goo just to go out into the cold cruel world was never easy. That day at least there was some hope. I had a great night planned. Of course there were a few speed bumps on the way to happiness, but at least happiness was actually out there on the horizon. I could just make out the topsail of the ship in the distance.

I rummaged through my closet and found the least offensive pair of "nice" jeans, which happened to be my favorite pair. I hate stereotypes, but I am very much a boy when it comes to laundry. Unless there's a stain or it actually smells bad, what's the point of washing it? Why wash something after one use if you didn't even so much as sweat in it? I get washing the underwear and socks, fine, and normally wear those only once, but with jeans and sweaters, come on. I slid into my new shirt and took a moment to appreciate the craftsmanship and stitching even though I knew it was most likely a programmed machine doing the work. Someone still had to program it and so I saluted the programmer. A few quick product applications to my hair, a few rogue hair plucks, and I was off. I had debated whether or not to get ready for my dinner with Nicole before I went to see Allison, but figured that I might not make it on time the way Allison liked to talk.

On the way to Allison's I tried thinking about what was happening with my life, constructing a timeline in my head and adding footnotes here and there. Was I so defeated by Allison that I so quickly dismissed her? For the first time it occurred to me that maybe it was possible that I was in some way glad that she rejected me. So much for my watery cleansing, I thought, as the cynical side of me raised an eyebrow, as if to say I told you so. "Nothing is ever as easy as it seems," it said and smiled a Grinchy smile.

I'm not prepared for this, I thought, as I rang Allison's doorbell. When I heard the Satan run and try to attack me through the door, it put me fully back in my place. I hand rang the doorbell out of respect, though I had a key, so I just went in after a few knocks as I always did—ready in my best Kung Fu stance in preparation for battle with the devil dog.

He was nicer than usual and just growled at me as I made my way through the kitchen to Allison's room. She was on the computer instant messaging with a friend. "Awww...that's so great" she said before noticing me and she clapped her hands lightly a few times. "What's so great?" I asked. Allison leapt out of her chair in pure terror before settling down into a frustrated laughter.

"You scared the shit out of me." She said as she tried to find her breath again.

"I know I can see it on your chair."

"Stop it, that's gross."

"You said it."

Off to a great start, I thought.

"What's so great on there?"

"Oh. My friend who desperately needs to find a nice guy said that she may have met one."

"Great!" I said trying to sound genuinely excited as I dropped myself on her bed taking count of how many bounces I managed to hit. Three.

"She had some rough times with the last guy that she was with and I was hoping she'd meet someone great soon. What are you doing here? I've been trying to call you."

"Yeah, I know. Sorry about that. I've just been having a really hard time with all of this, you know?"

She did know. I could tell that she wasn't doing so great herself. She looked tired and it made me realize the impact that I actually had on her life. She was worried about me. After a moment of silence I said, "I just needed some time to think about everything. I was pretty devastated when you said no."

"I never actually said no." But even as she said it I could tell she knew what was wrong with what she said. Saying 'can we talk about it?' is pretty much the same thing as saying 'no' and she knew it. "Ok," She continued, "so that's not the best response to a proposal. I guess I just wasn't expecting it and didn't know what else to do."

"You could have just said yes," I said. "But then what fun would that be, right?"

"Josh. I just feel like I have so much to do before I think about getting married. Do you know what I mean?"

"Oh sure, yeah. I totally understand," I retorted in my best sarcastic voice. I extended my body over her bed laying myself back with my hands behind my head imagining that I was on a hammock. What could be wrong with the world when you're on a hammock? Every time I've been in a hammock it was an immensely relaxing experience. I must have looked as if I were trying to calm myself down because Allison asked me "Where did you go?"

"I'm in a hammock on a beach in the Caribbean. I'd appreciate it if you didn't block my sunlight." I must have smiled unusually because she started to tense up.

"Why do you always just block this out?"

"Why do you always force me to try and block things out?" I didn't mean to hurt her, but I could tell by the silence that she felt as if a million tiny men suddenly built a scaled version of the great wall down the center of the room, splitting us apart. I took a moment of silence for the tiny men who died building the wall.

Allison shook her head. I didn't see her, of course, because I was swinging in the breeze of a Caribbean beach, but I could feel her shift her weight as she shook her head. You know what they say about a butterfly flapping its wings on the other side of the world? The same applies to a girl shaking her head in disappointment. The damage may be less significant—instead of a hurricane it's heartache—but depending on who you ask, both could be equally negative.

"You don't even realize how hard it was for me to get up the stones to ask you, do you? Let alone the money that I dropped on the goddamn ring."

"I never asked for a ring, Josh."

Oh yeah, I thought. If I asked you and didn't have a ring, instead of saying 'maybe', you would have just wondered where's the goddamn ring as you accidentally pushed me over the side of the Ferris wheel. The biggest lie a girl will ever tell you is that the size or authenticity of an engagement ring doesn't matter to her. The truth is that the worth of a woman could be defined by her engagement ring. When the future wife of a celebrity or millionaire shows off her ring, she's not showing how wealthy her husband is so much as proving how much she's worth to him. How much would you pay for me to be yours forever? That's a question every woman whispers into her loved one's ear as he sleeps, in hopes of one day proudly showing off the biggest rock to all of her friends.

As if she heard my thoughts she said, "Josh, it was...is a beautiful ring."

"But just not for you, right?" At this point I was cranky and on the verge of wanting a fight.

"I didn't say that one day this wouldn't have been wonderful, but I'm just not ready for this right now."

"So what now, then?"

"I don't know. I'd love to keep things how they were for now until I'm ready to move things forward."

After a dramatic pause I finally said, "I'm just not sure if I can do that."

The words hung in the air like a virus waiting to infect its next victim in order to propagate its species. The sickness finally entered her body, forcing her eyes to spill their reservoir of tears down her face. I realized then that I really didn't want to hurt her. I was still so bruised from the other night that I thought I wanted revenge, but seeing her depleted by my rejection felt bad. It was as if I was the dealer at a blackjack game and she was sitting at my table with nothing but a ten of hearts and a four of spades. She was addicted to the game and stuck in a bad spot with her last chip on the table ashamed of the possibility of going home broke. We sat there, dealer and nearly broke card player for a moment, aware of each other's roles in the game.

"What do you want to do?" she asked as if she really wanted to hear what I had to say.

"I'm pretty hurt." I said truthfully, taking note of how we both responded. "I'm not really sure. Maybe we both need some space for a bit to figure out what we both need."

"You mean you want to take a break?"

"I can't see myself having any semblance of normalcy around you at this point," I said, adding points to my word-of-the-day usage scoreboard. (Thanks Dictionary.com.) She shot me a look as if I were about to stab her in the chest. "Did you really think that we could just go on as normal?" clearly already knowing the answer.

"I guess I did."

"I just don't think that I can work that way, Allison. I put everything on the line the other night. Everything."

A monsoon started in her eyes. I'd never seen her cry that way before and for a minute my eyes were tempted to commiserate with her, but I convinced them to follow my orders, not hers. I got up from my hammock and made my way back to her to put an arm around her and pat her back. Not two arms for a full hug, just one—I was still too pissed to give her the real deal.

For a while we sat there speaking more of our feelings, though everything that really needed to be said was already said. Everything after that point was just talking about our emotions. Nothing could have been changed. Minds were made up, hearts were broken, then mended, feelings were hurt and healed again. The true strength of the human spirit is the resilience that it gets with change. We can adapt to so much and adjust so quickly to our surroundings. Eventually, when I couldn't take any more, I told her that I had to go. It took a few more minutes for me to make it down to the door, complete with the devil dog staring me down as usual. When I opened the door, ready for my escape, she scrounged up what few words she could and said, "So what if I had said yes? Where would we be now?"

"Probably happily planning a wedding," I said as I walked out the door just in time to make it to my date.

6

I got to the restaurant a few minutes early thanks to the 'T' and the chilly air. People from other parts of the country think that Northeasterners are always rushed, but really we're just cold. Those southern Californians have it easy, and so of course they mill around in the constant perfect seventy degree weather with a soft ocean breeze, walking inland as fast as they would be walking beach-bound. We hate them every second we hear them complain about a day of rain and are dumbfounded at their ignorance of what everyone else endures.

I took a seat at the bar and decided a drink would do me good. "Jack on the rocks please." I said in a grateful voice. "To love," I said quietly to myself raising my glass to an invisible crowd, though I'm pretty sure the guy next to me raised his glass as I said it. A world full of broken hearts, I thought. That's all this is. I wondered, as I sipped my drink, if there was anyone above the age of say, 18, in the world who hadn't had their hearts broken at some point. I thought about the statistical probabilities and realized that the percentages favored the broken hearted and I felt my spine curl forward a little into a slump. The only truly universal feeling, I thought. Maybe it's not love that unites the world, but rather it's broken hearts.

I felt a gentle tap on my shoulder and a whisper in my ear. "Hey." My barstool swung around to greet the voice. But it was more than just a voice. It took me a moment to muster up a simple 'hey' back. My God she looked unbelievable. There must be some secret ritual where they teach girls how to really dress up for something. Girls you'd see at regular times that didn't do much for you would suddenly be goddesses from a change in makeup, cut of a top, length of a skirt, or curl of a hair. Each girl must have had a private lesson on the art of alluring a boy at some point before the 8th grade. Nicole must have certainly taken diligent notes at her lesson. I forgot everything I learned about talking to girls, but managed enough small talk to not seem like an idiot.

I downed the rest of my drink and we made our way to the hostess, telling her that our party had arrived, and we were shown to our seats. I had been there once before with Allison, though it was something I tried not to think about so as to not ruin any positive feelings. Allison and I had gone there the first week we dated in college. It's one of the few restaurants I've seen that is both romantic and pretty cheap. It became a mainstay for college kids wanting to impress, but not wanting to break the bank. It was where I first learned most of Allison's history: how she was studying to be a physical therapist, the dog that she couldn't wait to move up to Boston when she got out of the dorms, her childhood and family life. It's amazing how much you can find out about a person at one dinner.

Nicole and I were seated at a table in a remote corner of the restaurant that was made for a new couple. The speakers were close enough to be able to recognize the songs, but far enough away that we could speak at a normal volume without strain. The worst place to be with someone you want to learn about is where you have to yell to be heard.

We ordered a bottle of wine, picking a Pinot Grigio that stood out, hoping for the best. I certainly wasn't a huge wine drinker and she said she wasn't really either, but it seemed like the best thing to try—something cold and refreshingly fruity. After the Jack and a glass of wine I finally felt like I had loosened up a bit. "How was class today?" I asked.

"It was alright—nothing too exciting. How was the rest of your day?"

"About the same," I said with a smile, "until now." I love making girls blush. "Have you been here before?"

"No, but I've always wanted to. A friend of mine told me that I have to try their duck confit."

"Their what?" My face probably asked it better.

"It's a duck leg. See," she pointed across the table at my menu, "they have it as an appetizer or as an entrée with risotto."

"You can even order it with the macaroni and cheese."

"I know what I'm getting," she said with a quiet clap of her hands.

"Well I guess I'll have to try it with the risotto, unless you're willing to let me try some of yours."

"No way! Get your own." She said with playful force.

The lingering thoughts of Allison had just about been masked by the time we ordered our entrées.

A quick look around could tell you that this was not the kind of place where meaningless chatter took place. Everyone there was either in love or on the path to it. I wondered if this was too much. It was only two days ago that Allison had rejected me and only an hour since we last spoke having left things in a limbo—where our thoughts and feelings could roam freely like animals liberated from long captivity.

I drifted in and out of the moment, not out of boredom but rather a hopeless longing for something positive to feel. For the most part I just let her talk. The sound of her voice was a refreshing reprieve from what I was used to. When you near the end of a relationship, anything that your partner says can be construed as negative, bringing a gloomy sky over the both of you that can't blow over. Nicole's voice circled me like a coven of witches, casting a spell on me that would last as long as she wished. There was no end to her spell as I watched her lips form words I could hear but didn't pay attention to. It wasn't that I didn't care about what she was saying, but that watching her lips form the words was enough for me. What other meaning or purpose could there be other than the simple beauty of their creation?

By the time our main course arrived, we were on our second bottle of wine and absurdly hungry. "I think it's your turn for a toast." I announced confident in my wording. She sat for a moment rummaging around her head for just the right words to say. I sat patiently awaiting whatever poetry she came up with.

"To Josh, may his life work itself out in a way that allows me to find my place in his story."

I felt my head melt down into my chest. She started to speak as if to apologize, but I gently raised a hand to stop her and said "I could only wish for such a story in my dreams."

Reality TV would have paid handsomely to get a moment like the one we just had on tape. We just stared at each other for a good minute, almost daring each other to be the first to look away. We sat there trapped between worlds we were leaving and worlds we were about to walk into. Nicole had her baggage—from a trip that lasted too long on a flight that didn't even serve peanuts or soda. I had my own baggage that I hadn't checked at the counter yet. We were both there waiting at the gate for a flight that had been delayed for years and wondered when it might take off.

While we shifted around in our chairs in preparation to finally eat, I stopped looked down at my plate with bewilderment. "What is it?" Nicole asked. I picked up my duck leg as if it were a sword being unsheathed and held it en guarde towards Nicole. After a short hesitation, she did the same and we laughed.

"Well, you certainly have me trying new things," I said as the laughter started to slow.

"Hopefully there will be many new things for us."

The conversation kept going with another bottle of wine as we took turns eating and talking, stopping occasionally here and there for an extra bite or two.

We debated a coffee or perhaps a tiramisu, but decided to head out into the world as our dessert. The lights of Boston at night were enough to fill any appetite left over after a meal. The check came and went before I even noticed how much the meal was, but I really didn't care. So I lost my job and have no actual income, who cares? A quick, slight bow from the waiter and we were off.

We drifted a little as we walked, leaving a curvy trail of shoe skids and high heel divots along the sidewalk like a flattened golf ball. We walked down Mass Ave out to the Harvard Bridge where I had spotted her earlier that day. Time had moved so slowly between our goodbye at the bridge that morning and our hello at dinner. I tried to take a good look at her without her noticing, but of course she noticed. "What do you think you're doing?" she said as she caught my wandering eyes. "I'm just trying to take as much of you in as I can."

She had to stand up on her toes a little, even in heels, but she tossed her arms around my neck and looked me right in the eyes. "So what do you think?"

"I think that you can't possibly be real." Only after a few drinks could I turn into a smooth talker. Had no wine or Jack been involved I probably would have said something like "I like it a lot." So hot. She pressed her body as close to me as she could so that I could feel her chest against mine and whispered, "Do I feel real enough now?"

Who are you, I thought, and how did you end up here on this bridge with me? It was clear what was supposed to happen next, but part of me couldn't do it. I'd never cheated on anyone before and wasn't sure if I was ready to be that guy. "Nicole," I said, regretting speaking almost immediately, "there are few things I would enjoy more than kissing you here right now—"

"So do it."

7

There had been no greater kiss in my life than the one I experienced there in the chilly glow of the headlights and taillights along Harvard Bridge. It echoed around in my skin, burrowing its way deeper into my marrow and shaking me from the inside. Her lips were soft and smooth, ripe with the delicious, sweet and bitter taste of wine. I reached my hand up to the back of her neck, running my fingers through her hair close to the skin and I felt her melt and drip like wax all over my body.

The moment lasted for a while as if we were in a movie: The camera spun in a circle around us like the sun as seen by a revolving planet. A dramatic, chunky indie-rock beat sped up with our heart beats as the camera continued to rotate around us. She was the first to retreat–slowly. My eyes stayed shut for a few moments after she had opened hers, hoping I wouldn't have to open them. I had to remind my lips to shut as I finally opened my eyes.

"Walk me home?" she asked softly.

"Of course."

We walked briskly back across the bridge to the Cambridge side and I made a mental note to take the bus home. We didn't say much on the walk back. I imagined that she was playing back the evening in her mind, fast-forwarding through the parts that could be edited out and rewinding over and over the highlights. I did the same, but probably had different notions of what the best parts were. Most of mine were just looking at her.

For the first time in a long while, I didn't think about what this may have meant for me. My analytical mind was usually clocked in, didn't take vacations and never needed much sleep. I didn't think about what this meant for Allison. I didn't think about what I would need to tell her. I didn't think about how she would react. I didn't think about The Unholy One relentlessly taking me down on her orders. I didn't even think about the fact that I had no job or any prospects in getting a new job. All I cared about was walking Nicole home with the hope of another kiss.

We rounded the corner of her street before she broke the silence. "I know it's the most common thing you could possibly say after a first date, but I really did have a great time. You are so sweet."

I wasn't really sure what to say so I just looked at her and said "I had a great time too."

Then she said shyly, but devilishly, "Do you want to come in for another drink or some coffee?"

I smiled and let out a little laugh.

"What?" she asked.

"There is nothing that I would love more than to come in, but I really don't think that either of us is prepared for what could happen in there. Let's not get too ahead of ourselves, ok?"

"Who are you, Josh?"

"I was hoping you could tell me."

We both smiled and she leaned up against me. She was standing one step up, so we were almost at eye level. Again she kissed me, with as much passion as the first.

"Good night, Josh," she said with a hint of disappointment in her voice.

"Good night," I said as she turned around and went up the steps to the front door and unlocked it. She turned her head slightly around before going in and I waited until the door shut before starting my way home.

The bus stop was just a block away. I walked, almost skipping, across the street to the bus stop and sat down. The air was much colder now, without the warmth of Nicole's body. For whatever reason, Allison popped into my head and I remembered our first kiss. Was it as powerful as this? I tried to remember. Did I feel this way back then? It made me wonder if the feeling I have now would ever leave. Damn you Allison, I thought, for ruining this moment.

By the time the bus came I had already decided that it would be unfair for this passion to ever fade. Eventually it would. It always does. After the first kiss, each subsequent kiss would be less and less special until it became a habitual act instead of a treasured moment. This was true of so many things, I thought, wishing that I had come to a different realization on the bus heading back home. Why should we ever continue anything, I thought, if the first parts are the best? The initial rush of life as things are fresh is the best part. Wouldn't that eventually go away? Is there any way to prevent it? If not, what is the point?

By the time I got home, I was so depressed by the theories my mind had concocted that I had lost my focus on how wonderful the night had really been. All I could think about was that eventually Nicole would become like Allison and she'd feel so comfortable with the way things were that she wouldn't want to move forward anymore. What a shitty way to end the night, I thought, as I brushed my teeth. When I finally laid down into bed, I tried to change my perspective. I thought maybe with some people it never fades. You hear about couples that have been married for 20 years and they're just as much in love as the day they met. I wondered if maybe they were lying, like politicians, for the good of the community. Maybe people will think that it's possible if we say it is.... And that is how I fell asleep.

I woke up with a slight hangover. Like a moron I didn't drink any water the whole night, just Jack and wine. Then I thought it was more likely because my body was tired from my mind working out all goddamn night. Sometimes I wondered what it would be like to not be so thoughtful, to not take on every problem placed in front of me, to not have to answer my own questions like it was a debate.

I got in the shower and started to think about Allison again. She is going to be devastated when I tell her about all of this. She has to have realized by this point, though, what she got herself into when she said no. Did she expect me to just wait around until she was ready? I put my whole life on the line and into her hands and she smeared the line and spread her fingers, letting me fall through like grains of sand. I wondered what would have happened if I had met Nicole 3 months later. Would it have been as exciting? Would I still have felt so guilty after formally breaking it off with Allison?

I realized that most of these questions had no answer. So when I got out of the shower, I made myself some coffee and decided that I should figure out at least one answer to the many questions of my life: I needed a job. That was the way my mind worked. Find one correct answer and let the rest disappear. So I stole the neighbor's newspaper and went to the job listings page wondering if that section still existed in the age of the Internet. Sure enough, there it was, and so I went through and circled ones that I thought might suit me.

Most of them were data entry jobs that I figured would soon be filled by software. The occasional fun one would pop up, but was normally already taken by the time the ad was printed. The cool places around town somehow filled positions before actually having them available, as if there were some waiting list that people get on for the next available slot.

I remembered that the day before, Nicole had told me to look into doing music reviews, and after she mentioned it again last night I felt as though there was no reason not to. Unfortunately the Globe had nothing of the sort to offer me. That is certainly one of the jobs with a waiting list, I thought, as I moved on to other ideas and decided to try an old-fashioned way of looking for a job.

I made my way down past Allston Beat, JP Licks, Newbury Comics and all the other hip places. But even the usually under-staffed Trident Booksellers didn't have anything for me. I walked the street just as I did yesterday, but without the deep electronic score of stacked sine waves, pops and clicks. I looked in every storefront I walked by for a "Wanted" sign, but no luck. I was getting nervous that no one actually did that anymore. TGI Fridays didn't need a bartender. Tealuxe didn't need any servers. All the chic restaurants I wouldn't have a chance at with my goofy haircut and couple of visible tattoos. I made a pact with myself to apply for the first Wanted sign that I saw.

Desperation set in as I turned around at the Commons. There has to be something out there, I thought. Another Starbucks probably wouldn't hire me after what happened. And I didn't want to work at a different coffee shop and have to re-learn some other way of making coffee. I felt like a foot soldier doing reconnaissance disguised as a civilian—finding out what businesses we could hide our soldiers in for the right time to strike. But the mission was looking to be a bust.

I rounded the corner back onto Mass Ave, and there it was—the butt of jokes for college kids around the city. A Wanted sign had just gone up in the window of Sweet and Nasty. I could see the woman who had just planted the sign there turn around to head back in. You have got to be kidding me, I thought to myself. The sign wasn't there on my way here. Someone wanted me to wait until I had no hope left. That way it wouldn't seem so bad because, hey, I found something. Along with selling candies shaped like phalluses and sex toys, their small shop made adult-themed cakes. Customers had their choice of a big cock, a set of hooters, or even offered a woman's crotch, complete with 'furry' chocolate shavings.

I'm sure every college kid in the city at some point had a taste of a giant penis cake. They were a mainstay of 21st birthday parties, gay pride socials, and girl's nights out. After taking a moment to think of the absurdity of applying for, let alone getting, the job, I forced myself to walk in. I'd never actually been inside the place, but I had walked by it so many times that I felt as though I had. When I made my way through the door, I saw the lady that put the sign up was writing some words with frosting onto a giant penis cake. "What's that one going to say?"

She smiled wryly and said, "Happy fucking birthday, slut."

"Classic," I mumbled.

HOW TO DISAPPEAR COMPLETELY

She just nodded, as if to say what else can you say really?

"So I just noticed that you put up that Help Wanted sign."

"You think you'd be good at this?"

"Well what all is involved in the job?"

"We make all the cakes here, though you wouldn't have to do that part, at least for now. You'd be required to do a lot of random things, there is normally only one of us on the floor at a time. Someone is in the back making the cakes, but someone has to be out here for all the walk-in customers. You'd have to write on the cakes, answer the phones, take orders, and keep the place tidy. It's actually a good bit of work."

"Do you like it?"

"Yeah it's alright, they pay pretty well, considering what you're doing."

"Well I may as well fill out an application, right?"

"Full time or part time."

"Probably full time," I guessed was the right answer.

"Great, we could definitely use the help."

The application was just basic information. I always wondered how anyone could figure a person out by an application. The interview is really what makes or breaks a hire. Most employers say that they can tell within 10 seconds of someone walking in the door whether they have the job. 10 seconds. That goes for high-level jobs as well as the Burger Kings.

"Who's the manager here?"

"Her name is Karen. She doesn't come by very often, but if she likes your résumé, she'll come in for an interview."

"So should I just bring this back to you then?"

"Or whoever is working at the time."

"Great, thanks." I turned around before deciding that I should be more cordial. "I'm Josh, by the way."

"Carrie," she said smiling as if to say Sorry, unable to shake a hand or high five because she was covered in frosting. Clearly she didn't normally do the lettering on the cakes. "Well hopefully I'll see you here again when I get the job." I could feel some of the excess confidence get stuck in my throat like phlegm from a cold. The bell of the door cued my exit and I stepped back out into a world where penises weren't made of butter, sugar, eggs and flour.

When I got home, I tossed the solitary application onto my desk so that it could at least be nearby some other paper goods. Even though they probably didn't speak the same language, they could at least smile and nod to each other every now and again reaffirming each other's existence like strangers in a coffee shop.

Glancing at the computer, I noticed that I had an instant message from Nicole waiting for me.

nickylox85: hey you, what r you up to today?

I wondered how long ago the message was left, but it didn't say. Then I thought about what she may have said if she were with me on my quest that day. Would she have laughed at the notion of Sweet and Nasty or maybe been repulsed. I debated telling her at all, but decided to not start building our relationship on lies.

jbone1492: i was out looking for a job all day.

I replied, wondering if she was actually there still or had moved on. I waited to see if there was a response, but after a minute or so I figured she was doing other things. I grabbed a pen, pulled the cap off and started my way through the Sweet and Nasty application. All the basic information came easily, without need for reference. Occasionally I pulled out some old phone numbers of bosses, who probably didn't work at my old employers anymore, but I had to put down something. I debated whether or not to include Marcus and Starbucks, but I had been there for the last few years and decided that I'd better. Despite how I was let go, Marcus would be nice to whoever called and say that I was let go for some benign reason. I had given him years of quality work. The least he could do was to help me move on.

Every detail of my employment history (that I wanted them to know about) was once again on paper for someone else to judge me on. It was a cruel system, especially for those who didn't look good on paper. But I guess it was even crueler in the first 10 seconds of an interview for those who didn't look good in person. I've got decent marks on both, I thought, and folded the paper hot dog style placing it in view next to my computer monitor.

My computer chimed informing me that I had received an instant message. It was Nicole again.

nickylox85: that's great ☺ and?

jbone1492: i was hoping to find some sort of job in the paper for writing, but i couldn't find any. then i ended up walking down newbury looking for help wanted signs.

nickylox85: lol that's funny. did you find anything?

jbone1492: i did grab one application, but it's kind of a weird place.

nickylox85: it's not condom world is it?

jbone1492: haha no not that weird I suppose. close. one more guess.

nickylox85: umm..

jbone1492: they do have some risqué stuff, but it's mostly edible...

nickylox85: no way. sweet & nasty?

jbone1492: ha, yeah.

nickylox85: my girlfriends got me a cake from there the other night before we went to our house.

jbone1492: which one?

nickylox85: it was a cake in the shape of a penis with frosting at the tip.

jbone1492: ha, it's the details that count.

nickylox85: it was more detailed than that, but we'll leave some of the details unsaid.

jbone1492: fair enough.

nickylox85: what are you doing later?

jbone1492: nothing really planned, why?

nickylox85: i was just thinking maybe we could hang out.

jbone1492: i'd love to, what do you want to do?

nickylox85: some guys are having a party over here at school. maybe we could go to that?

jbone1492: i haven't been to a college party in a few years.

nickylox85: haha that's ok, i'm sure they're the same as you remember.

Except I hated most college parties that I went to.

jbone1492: sure we can do that.

nickylox85: great do you just want to meet me at my place beforehand? i'll cook us some dinner.

jbone1492: i'll be there. i just need to shower and get a few things taken care of before i leave.

By that I meant I had to mull around on the computer and catch up with my social networking sites a bit.

nickylox85: no problem, see you later. ☺

I signed off from iChat and logged onto Myspace and then Facebook to stalk a few people. I had occasionally checked out Allison's page to see what she'd been up to that I hadn't heard about. It's amazing what you can find out about a person from their friends' comments on their page. Nothing of worth showed up this time, so I logged off and turned on the shower. I thought about Nicole as I shampooed my hair, but by the time I got to washing my body my thoughts had drifted to Allison. Was her rejection really enough to bring another relationship into my world and let ours die stillborn? I clearly still loved her, but this story that I started with Nicole was beginning to be too exciting to put down. I just kept wanting to read on to find out what happens next. With Allison, I felt like we had enough words between us to justify calling our story a novel and publishing it with its ending as is. Maybe in another life there could have been a sequel, but there would have to be more demand for it to happen.

I dried myself off with a towel that I noted should be tossed into the laundry soon. Wiping the steam off of the mirror I revealed my face but felt uneasy about looking at myself because I felt guilty. And it finally started to hit me how I was just making things worse by not telling Allison about Nicole. The longer I waited, the more inappropriate it got. On the other hand I thought it would be premature to give up Allison completely before I knew if I wanted to take on Nicole for a long-term thing. But doesn't that mean that I don't want Allison?

I read somewhere that people are getting too picky about their mates. Now, in a world where people more than ever are being able to marry whom they want instead of for dowry or social status, the freedom to make choices means the freedom to unmake them as well. I'm not saying that we should go back to those times, but I do think people need to stop searching for perfection in a mate before settling down. I don't believe there is one perfect mate for every one person. In fact, you pair up almost any man and any woman and you will eventually get children out of it. Love? Who knows? But at least happiness in a life together.

People have always had affairs, but it was less talked about. Today if you cheat on someone they'll most likely find out any number of ways. Suddenly you put a new, unfamiliar face in your top friends on a social networking site and you have earned instant suspicion. It's a brutal time for love in this world. What does that mean for me, I thought. Am I just throwing away something great with Allison for the thrill of a new start with someone else? Will Nicole become just as commonplace as Allison? How long can things really stay fresh in any relationship?

Those thoughts plagued me as I picked out what to wear for the evening. College parties were always so lame for me, though that was mostly because I was so shy. If people didn't come up to talk to me, I ended up not talking with anyone and would drink until I had the courage to go up and talk to somebody. Anybody. Things will be different now with Nicole, I thought. I already have someone to talk to. I finally looked at myself and said, "You're ready."

8

As we walked up to the club where the party was, I started to wonder what was going on. I heard a band bumping some up-tempo swing and as if on cue Nicole said "You're going to love this." Everyone outside the place was dressed up like a hipster from various eras. There were girls dressed as 20s flapper girls. There were the jive cats from the 40s complete with pinstripe zoot suits, wide brimmed hats and long double chains. There were the 50s kids with their ducktails, pressed jeans and rolled up short sleeve shirts. I realized then that I was in for something way outside of my comfort zone. "Why didn't you tell me to dress any differently?" I asked, suddenly feeling obscenely naked and self-conscious. I am Adam and Nicole is my apple. I have sinned, I thought.

"I really don't think that I'm going to fit in here," I screamed, trying to be heard above the jive sounds, as we walked in the door. "Relax, you'll be fine!" she yelled back. "Come on let's get you a drink to loosen up!" I looked at the dance floor over my left shoulder as we walked towards the bar. Some girl had just been flung into the air as if she were one of those little plastic parachute-adorned soldiers, only the person who threw her was a sadistic son of a bitch and cut the parachute off before he tossed her. I cringed and turned away with my eyes closed waiting for the thump of her body on the ground. Nothing. I turned back around and her feet were over her head as if she jumped high off the ceiling trying to touch the floor with her head.

"Can we get a whiskey on the rocks and a whiskey sour?" Nicole blared to the bartender, who I'm sorry to say, was not wearing a bolo. Nicole looked back at me as I stared out over the dance floor with my jaw on the floor and a look of sheer terror stapled to my face. "Better make that a double whiskey!"

"Listen to that band," she said, "aren't they amazing? Have you heard music this great before?"

I was still in too much shock from the whole thing to respond.

"Here, drink this." She said as she handed me a double whiskey.

I downed the whole thing in a few gulps and as any good woman would, she immediately got me another. Before she handed me the second she said "Before I give you this, you have to promise me that you'll at least try and learn some basic steps so that we can dance at some point when you're done being amazed, loosen up and start enjoying the whole thing, ok?"

I responded with a double nod, my jaw still on the floor.

"Good, then here you go."

I took the drink, closed my eyes, took a deep breath and tried to open them with a fresh perspective. Everyone there had something that made them cool. Their clothes, their moves, or their general 'I don't give a shit' demeanor. The band stopped their song with a whirl of whining trumpets and an amazing drum solo. They really were good, I thought, if nothing else, I'll just enjoy the band. It was rare to see this kind of music in this city, let alone in this decade. Who knows, though, I thought, maybe this happens every night in a different place and I just have no idea.

Glancing towards Nicole, trying to make it seem like I wasn't looking at her, I noticed that she was bobbing her head side to side to the beat as she sipped her drink through a stirring straw. I wondered why she didn't tell me what we were actually doing that night, but quickly realized that I very well may have said no. Seeing me watch her, she spoke up. "So what do you think?"

"It's pretty amazing."

She just smiled like a girl at her sweet sixteen. "Do you do this kind of thing a lot?"

"Whenever I can."

Of course you do, I thought somewhat despairingly. That meant that I had to be into it as well if I wanted to stay cool in her eyes. Maybe this is how people keep things fresh, by always doing new things. I finished my second drink and had finally started to loosen up a bit. I slammed my empty glass down on the bar and shook out my body like Donald Duck always did before he played golf in the old cartoons. Head to foot, just shook out all the bad. "So how does this work?"

Her eyes lit up with absolute joy. I will always remember those eyes. "You really want to try it?"

"Let's do it."

She snatched my hand almost pulling it off my arm and led me to a less crowded corner. It was nearly impossible to hear her yell out footsteps over the music, but I listened, watched, and tried to catch on. Step, step, rock-step, step step rock-step. It's a hard dance for any musician that doesn't dance. They counted steps in three when the song was in 4 and it drove me nuts, I kept trying to add in another step on 4, when I was supposed to go back to one.

Step, step, rock-step, step, step, rock-step. It became my mantra as I tried to tune out the beat and just step my mantra in time. At one point I closed my eyes using Nicole to steady my tipsy body from capsizing.

"I think you're starting to get it!" she exclaimed with a grin the size of Montana.

I didn't say anything in return, I just kept practicing my mantra and hoped my feet followed. I really was starting to get it and after a while the steps seemed to somehow make sense. "No one else is doing this, though." I noticed.

"This is just the beginning. You ready for another one already?"

"I'll try."

She led me through another few steps that actually made sense with the music. She called it the Charleston. Back left, front left, front right, front back, and step. I loved this one. "See we can do this one facing each other or I can follow your feet and stand next to you." By then the warm tingle of the 4 whiskeys was starting to reach every inch of my body and I really felt the music. It was unlike anything I had every experienced before. I actually felt connected with the music. Before it was an intruder in my brain and by now it was my best friend. The piano player took a solo and I was completely engulfed inside the Charleston until the song finished and the joint erupted into cheers.

In the next song she showed me a few more moves and taught me how to lead her, though really most of the night she was doing most of the leading. She taught me how to do a few moves where I spun her around and then how to combine all of them. I was panting from exhaustion and sweating through my shirt from all this movement that my body wasn't used to.

After another jumpin' tune, the place suddenly exploded with applause as the band played the first few notes of the next number. It took a few more notes for me and I belted out "I know this one!" excited that I actually knew a piece that apparently everyone else did as well. Before I knew it, Nicole had ushered me out to the middle of the dance floor dodging the flying feet and flailing arms. "Go Daddy-O" everyone yelled as we got to the center of the floor. I felt as though all of the lights in the place had suddenly been pointed at me and the band stopped for a moment for everyone to look at the new kid in despair. After making sure my balls were still there, I said fuck it and started dancing. The lights must have moved again and the band started playing again because suddenly I blended in with everyone else, raising my arms and changing on every cue of "Go Daddy-O," never missing a step.

By the end of the song I nearly collapsed. Seeing my limp body and feeling sorry for me Nicole said "Hey, do you want to get some air for a minute."

She took my red, sweaty face as a Yes and led us towards the exit. Everyone in the place slowed down into a sexy mambo as we went out and let the cool New England evening air freeze the sweat that covered my upper body. I didn't care if I'd get pneumonia, for the moment it felt great.

"I think you got it." She chuckled.

I couldn't help but to laugh as well and said, "I don't think I could say that I 'got' anything, but I might be 'getting' it."

"Fair enough." she said as we sat down on the second step. It was too bad that neither of us smoked, because I'm sure in the script of our story that existed somewhere we would be having cigarettes now. That seemed to be the norm for this crowd. Booze, jazz and cigarettes. Again I laughed, loud enough to make Nicole notice.

"What?" she asked.

"I was just thinking how out of place I must look here. Seriously why couldn't you have told me to dress cooler?" She looked at me with a look that seemed to say 'you have clothes like this?' Seeing that reaction, I felt as though I should redeem myself. "I could have at least thrown together something a little bit more convincing than this." I tugged on my button-down dress shirt. "Even jeans and a t-shirt would have been better, right?"

"Oh you look fine. No one here cares what you're wearing, they're just here to have a good time."

She was probably right. Most people there were in their own little worlds, whether it was a world of one or a world of two, everyone had their own place. (I even saw a world of three and commended the guy's stamina.) The band had started back into its regular fast-paced swing and I wondered whether the break into a slow mambo was for the dancers or for them. It had to be just as exhausting making the music as it was to dance to it. They put so much into playing the songs. I couldn't remember seeing another modern band work as hard or have as good a response from the crowd.

I had just caught my breath, when Nicole said "You ready to go back in?"

I wanted to say 'Are you serious? I just calmed down.' But of course instead I said "Sure" as I thought about how sore I was going to be the next day. We both got another drink by the bolo-less bartender and sat on the barstools marveling at the wonder and the energy of the place. I don't know how much more I can do, I wanted to say. I don't think I have much left in me. I decided against it, though, in the spirit of the moment as she pulled me back out to the floor. She started to do more of the leading and I let her more and more. After a while she was spinning me around instead of telling me to spin her around. I started to feel a little light-headed and wanted to go outside again, but she kept spinning me more and more and more and more, until eventually the whole room started to spin.

I woke up in the emergency room as the nurse was struggling to find a vein for the IV. Of course I couldn't have waited just one more minute until she was done stabbing me. That would have been too easy. A sharp groan announced my re-entry into the world as the needle finally found its way into the vein. "Good, you're awake," the nurse whispered, "I'll go get the doctor."

"What happened?" I mumbled groggily as one should in these situations.

"Hey Josh. How are you feeling?" Ah that soothing voice meant at least Nicole was still with me.

An "Ugh" was all I could muster up.

"You passed out at the club and I wasn't sure what else to do so we called an ambulance. Me and a few other guys kept trying to wake you up, but nothing was working. I'm so glad you're ok." She threw her arms around my neck and hugged me. My body was still a little sore from dropping so hard to the ground and I couldn't help but wince a little at the touch. She sensed my pain and quickly withdrew. The doctor walked in unimpressed with life and wishing I was a more interesting case. "Well," he was obliged to tell me, "it seems like you were just a little dehydrated and passed out. Too much jazz and booze and not enough water will do that." I silently applauded his attempt at befriending me, but it was already too late for that. "We just want to keep you here for a few more hours to make sure you're stable and then you can go."

"Great."

As he walked away I realized how much his "diagnosis," if you can call it that, would cost me. Please, tell me something that I couldn't have figured out on my own if I weren't passed out. Maybe then you'd be earning your salary. "You are dehydrated" does not warrant thousands of dollars in bills. For a moment then I got angry at Nicole for calling 911. How could you not realize that me passing out certainly did not require a hospital and an ambulance? I thought. I would have eventually woken up on the sidewalk and been able to walk home without worrying about too much else. Instead, I got to worry about hospital and doctor bills. Thanks.

Nicole, fully aware of the tension that cut the room in half, came over to the bedside. "Nicole, I appreciate your concern, but was the hospital really necessary?"

"I didn't know what else to do, you wouldn't wake up. We tried and tried for 15 minutes or so, but nothing. I was worried that you were really hurt."

Her face was too apologetic for me to blame. She was just doing what she thought was right. I couldn't be mad at her for this. It was my own fault. I closed my eyes, took a few deep breaths, and realized that it would all eventually be ok. I'd figure things out. "I guess it's about time to turn in that application, eh?"

Nicole let out a chuckle, which made me laugh, and soon we were both laughing out loud. For a minute there we had a sweet little moment, between the beeping on my heart rate and the distant sounds of death pulling the life out of a too-young woman down the hallway.

We sat there not knowing what to say for a while, just watching TV, before the nurse with the bad aim returned to wheel me out the front door as if I'd been in prison for 20 years. We walked to The Charles/MGH T stop and sat solemnly on a bench.

"I'm sorry I was unappreciative of all your help," I admitted. "I just don't have a whole lot of money right now and this is certainly not going to make life easy for a while."

"I know, I thought about that as we got out of the ambulance. I just saw you lying there limp on the ground like that and nothing I did was helping and I didn't know what else to do."

"I understand. Thanks." I said with a little smile.

"You're welcome. I'm just glad you're ok." She said with a bigger smile.

9

We, more specifically, I, decided that I should just head home for what was left of the night. Nicole walked me home for a change and we parted with a hug and a small kiss on the cheek. I was still groggy from the mild drugs they gave me at the hospital and couldn't handle much more than that. I made my way up to my room and fell directly onto my bed. I didn't bother taking off any more than my shoes and jeans before crawling my way under the covers. If it weren't for the latter part of the evening, I would have called tonight one of the best nights out that I'd had in a long while. I laid there for a minute recounting the events of the night and playing back in my head images of me actually dancing—swing dancing—to a live big band. Who was this girl and what was she doing to me?

Then I thought of Allison for a moment and wondered what her night was like. Was she still hoping that I'd come around and go back to her? I debated calling her to tell her that I had gone to the hospital, though I was ok, but I realized that it wasn't a real cause to go to the hospital and then I'd have to explain why I was at the club to begin with. I wasn't ready to go through that conversation yet. Soon, though, I thought as I drifted to sleep, my mind flitting between all the characters and scenes of my life, shifted and distorted into something that only my unconscious mind could understand.

The morning came all too quickly and without much warning as I woke up terrified. For a moment I couldn't think of why I was so terrified. My shirt and sheets were soaking wet from sweat and it took me a minute to escape from the watery clutches of my bed. As I yanked my sheets off the mattress, I remembered my dream in all its ghastly horror and dropped my sheets on the floor. I'll have to go talk to Nicole about it all and see what she had to say. I gathered the sheets back into a bundle and dropped them into a trash bag like a homeless Santa's toy sack. The shower had never felt so welcoming. The water hugged me as I stepped into the tub, rubbing my shoulders, patting my back and assuaging my nerves as a good friend would after a break up. 'There, there' it said to me as I cleaned myself from the night's workout on my body. Everything is going to be just fine.

As if healed by a small Chinese man's homegrown herbs, I felt completely rejuvenated after the shower. Stepping out on to the damp bath mat, I had never felt so good. Instead of the sense of doom I usually felt as I got ready for each day, I felt as though I had a purpose. I had a reason to be alive that day and it felt good. I even cooked breakfast, which I never did, and made the home version of a bacon, egg and cheese Mc Muffin. Breakfast normally only occurred with girls over or on special occasions, which were often one and the same.

The mostly blank Sweet & Nasty application was still resting on my desk like a bored cat waiting for some attention. The clock on my computer reminded me that I had just enough time to finish filling it out and head down there before the store opened its doors to the world. I bullshitted my way through most of the application, as any good lawyer might, guessing what their jury wants to hear. "Alright," I said as I signed and dated the bottom, then walked out the door.

☂

Carrie was there opening up the shop as I walked in the door. "Hey," I said as if we were already friends.

"Hey."

She must have had just as much of a rough night as I did because she looked terrible. It's amazing what a bad night's sleep and dehydration from alcohol can do to a person's appearance.

"So I brought this back in today."

"So I see."

"Should I just leave it with you, trusting that you'll get it to the top of the pile for me?"

"You sure you want to trust me with that?"

"Not really, but what other options do I have?" I said it in a way that was just nice enough to not sound mean, but could have still been construed as mean if someone chose to take it that way. "Actually," she added, "if you wanted to wait around a little while, Karen is coming down in about 20 minutes.

"Aren't I lucky then?"

A bland smile was her response.

"Do you want a coffee or something, I might go down to the Starbucks real quick if there's time." I said trying to be nice. "What kind of coffee does Karen drink?"

"You really want this job, neh?"

"I really want a job, yeah."

"It's hard to remember, you may want to write it down."

"I used to work there, I'm sure I can handle it."

"Suit yourself, she likes an extra hot, double half-caf, non-fat, no-whip mocha with soy milk."

I tried to keep my composure, but clearly I couldn't as I laughed. It boggled my mind to think that there were two people in the world, let alone in the city who would order that same drink.

"It's silly, right? But that's what she likes. I'll take a medium coffee."

"Sure no problem."

It was kind of exciting going to another Starbucks location. No one knew me there, but I felt as though I had some sort of connection with all of them, like distant cousins or adopted children, separated at birth into different families. I ordered three drinks, paid with a card and noted how nice everyone was there. This is a good store, I thought. I wondered what the manager was like. The drinks came a minute later and the guy gave me a tray without me even asking for one.

I thanked him and headed back up the street, rounded the corner and returned to 'The Nasty,' as I decided to nickname it, with the three coffee drinks. Out of my peripheral vision, I noticed that two people were now inside chatting. Great, she's here, I thought. As I walked in the door, my heart dropped to the floor like a Foosball at the beginning of a match ready to be kicked around. For a moment, I didn't think that she recognized me, but when she saw me carrying the Starbucks cups, it hit her. "You!" She said like a villain from a Disney movie, with a voice that could have easily been Cruella de Vil or Ursula. I felt her stare from 20 feet away like a flaming arrow on course to my heart.

This is just ridiculous, I thought, as I contemplated running out the door. What was the point of working for her? She'd do nothing but try and get me back, if she even hired me to begin with. I really need this, I said to myself as I walked up and handed her a drink. "I guess this one's on the house." I said trying to keep the mood light, as I handed Carrie her drink.

"It damn well better be, what are you doing here?"

I answered by raising up my application high enough for her to see.

"Are you serious?" she asked sternly.

"I guess I am."

"You think I'd actually hire you?"

"Maybe you're as desperate as I am."

"You can barely even make a drink right; what makes you think you could get anything right here?"

"To be fair, I doubt that anyone is as specific about their novelty cakes as they are about their coffee drinks."

She was clearly offended at the fact that I had both put her down as well as her business.

"Look," she huffed, "I have no intention of hiring you. I'll take this application and keep it just in case no one else applies, but you may as well keep looking elsewhere. You will be nothing but a worst case scenario, if that."

"Don't I get any points for remembering your drink? I can't be all that worthless if I can remember something so specific."

She took a sip and tried very hard not to enjoy it.

"Even if I gave you a few points for that, you'd still be far from breaking even, let alone having a good score."

I gave her the finger with my eyes.

"Carrie, it was nice to see you again. You're both welcome for the drinks."

As I pushed the door open, I heard the beginnings of her version of the Starbucks incident. I would have loved to hear her version to see how deranged I was in it. How deep into the circles of hell she wanted me to be sent. I would have loved to see Carrie's reaction to the whole thing, but alas it didn't seem to be my destiny. I ran a few numbers through my head to figure out a ballpark figure for the chances of her being the woman that I wanted a job from, and decided that I had a better chance of winning the lottery. On the walk back home, I stopped in at a corner store to buy a lottery ticket. Most people think that luck, whether good or bad, is a lot like lightning when operating on such small chances–that it doesn't come around more than once or twice a lifetime. I decided to find out for myself and put 20 bucks down to win on the Massachusetts Jackpot.

When I got home, an instant message from Nicole was waiting for me, as well as one from Allison. Oddly enough, they both said the same thing. "What are you doing today?"

I answered Nicole's first with a "hanging out with you?" Apparently that was the right answer.

nickylox85: good, maybe you could come over for dinner?

jbone1492: that sounds great, what time?

nickylox85: 5:30ish? you can help me cook.

jbone1492: should i bring anything?

nickylox85: just some whiskey if you want it. though after last night maybe that's not the best idea.

jbone1492: yeah, we'll see.

Though after the excitement at the cake shop today I felt like I could certainly use a good drink.

nickylox85: did you drop off that application?
jbone1492: i did, and you are never going to believe what happened.
nickylox85: what?
jbone1492: i'll just tell you tonight, alright?
nickylox85: ok, i have one more class to head to today. i'll see you tonight ok?
jbone1492: i'll be there.

She left as usual with a ☺ and put up an away message that said 'class, then josh ☺'. I certainly wasn't used to all the smiley faces, but supposed that I could get used to them. I had a few hours to kill and wondered what to do. Just for fun I decided to write. Remembering how amazing the band was the night before, I decided to write a mock review of the show. I tried to start without thinking too hard and just letting the words find their own way out of my fingertips.

I typed non-stop for a few minutes then leaned back in my chair and read it back aloud. This is actually pretty good, I thought, and decided to print it out to bring to Nicole. She was the bug carrying the spores of inspiration in my ear telling me to write, so she may as well get credit for it and see the fruits of it. Fortunately and unfortunately my review took only 15 minutes to write and I still had a few hours before leaving. I wondered how many websites there are that review shows and albums and how many of them may need freelance writers.

There were a surprising number of sites that raised their hands to Google's inquiry, so I picked out the most promising ones for further research. All of the few sites that I found had staff writers and surely didn't need any more. Then I tried to find a blog or two on the subject, resulting in more dismal prospects.

I didn't know the first thing about websites, but I thought that maybe I could start a blog of music reviews. If I wrote specifically for college kids, I could probably get a reputation going. My mind buzzed with ideas like a coffee shop full of beat poets—everyone vying to be heard as a fresh voice. I spent the rest of the afternoon looking into how to make it happen. I signed up with BlogSpot.com and set up my first blog. Boston Gig Reviews. I used my review of Wally and the Whale as the first post. With just enough time to shower, get ready, and head over to Nicole's, I sat back for a moment to marvel at my creation. I didn't create very often, nothing original at least. Coffee drinks, essays, some dumb, trite poetry were always part of my palette, but nothing as original as this. And as much as I loved music, I had never learned to write about it.

After hurriedly getting ready for the evening, I marched my way triumphantly over to Nicole's as if I had just been part of a military coup, ready for a new life. She opened the door, happy to see me, but her face wasn't quite as full of life as normal. Asking a girl if she's alright is like jaywalking across a black ice-covered 4 lane street: You think you can make it safely to the other side, but you're more likely to slip and fall to a most certain death. I was not in the mood to die. She kissed me blankly on the cheek and I thought how it may as well have been Allison. I decided that I'd better ask. "Are you ok?" I spat out hesitantly.

"Yeah, school was rough today."

"What happened?"

"Apparently my ex-boyfriend has been following me. Last night he was there at the club, watching us. Then he interrupted my class this afternoon and said some pretty terrible things, in front of everyone. My teacher ended up calling security and they escorted him out recommending that I get a restraining order. After class the campus security helped me fill out the paperwork and now he's not allowed within 50 feet of me."

"I don't know what to say. That's just awful."

I really didn't know what to say.

"I've never had to do anything like that before."

"Hopefully you never have to again."

I pulled her close to me and put my arms around her as her hands covered her face to shield me from view of tears. I'd learned a long time ago that often the best thing you can say is nothing. Instead, I offered the comfort of my arms for as long as she needed, stroking her long, soft strawberry blonde hair as she wept quietly. Eventually she calmed herself and pried her face away from my tear stained sweater. "I'm sorry." She said as if something were her fault.

"There is no way that this could be your fault."

"I just didn't mean to ruin the evening."

"Nothing is ruined. Let's get you a drink."

Suddenly my whole day seemed too pale in comparison, so I opted to not share until she was ready to ask. I thought that I would have sounded either like I was trying to make my morning seem worse than her incident, or my afternoon would have seemed like bragging. I made her a whiskey sour, poured myself a double on the rocks, and ushered her to a seat on the couch where we could relax for a minute. "It's all over now, let's just try and relax."

"Ok." She said horribly unconvincingly.

This was not going well. I had to think of the catalyst, the thing to turn the whole evening around, and fast. "I took your advice," I said hopefully, "I decided to start a music review blog."

Her face widened and mine lifted in response. "That's so great!" What are you going to review?"

"Well I was thinking of starting with the band from last night and then just go to shows and check bands out and then write about it. Maybe eventually they'll invite me to shows and stuff. I might try and keep it indie and local."

"That is a great idea. You already wrote something about last night?"

"It's actually already online."

"No way! Let me see it."

I navigated my way to the as yet undesigned blog and let her read the lonely review.

"This is so great." She smiled, "You should send this to the band. I'm sure they'd love it."

'I did it!' I thought. It worked. For the rest of the night we laughed, drank, cooked, and after I had a little more to drink she got me to learn a few more dance moves. I made her promise, though, that she'd make me drink more water and take more breaks if we ever went to another dance again, to which she gladly agreed. This is how a relationship should be, I thought: fun. We just had fun together. We could just hang out together and have plenty to talk about. There was so much to learn about each other and we wanted to learn it all. I waited for a while before telling her about what happened that morning and the absurdity of the coincidence that the fat bitch from Starbucks was also the manager of Sweet & Nasty. It hit me then that I'd probably have to start over on a job search. Even if they did call me back I wasn't entirely sure that I'd want to work for the woman who had actually gotten me fired from my previous job. I was tempted to apply at the Starbucks on Newbury, but figured that I wouldn't have a chance after being fired from another, unless I lied and didn't put that on my résumé. Then I'd just seem like a fast learner, which is never bad.

No, that would be stupid. The point in the evening came where a decision had to be made about the precarious sleeping arrangements of new lovers. Should I stay or should I go? I still wasn't sure if I was ready to make the plunge into a sexual relationship with Nicole as the guilt would be unbearable when I actually finally talked with Allison. So I made the decision to leave once again. She actually asked me to stay, but I explained why I had to leave which made her want me to stay even more.

The look in a girl's eyes when she wants you to follow her into her room and into bed for the first time is one of the few things that still makes me believe in God. It took every ounce of willpower and persuasion to convince myself to leave, but eventually I did and tried to think about how amazing it would be when I finally got to stay over. I walked home in a pleasant whiskey haze without a care in the world and later that night about Nicole and how things might play out on our first night together, whenever that would be.

About halfway home, with every few steps I felt as though someone was following me, though every time I turned around to look there was no one there. I had never felt so spooked by the silence or the air of a dark night before, and felt in my gut that something was wrong. After a few more minutes of that feeling coursing through my body, I suddenly felt the sharp sting of a blow to the back of my head. I didn't scream, though I was hit hard enough to make my eyes water. I felt around the back of my head with my hand but didn't find any blood. I turned around to see the outline of a manly figure through a watery blur.

The pain was enough to render my mind completely useless for a moment. Not thinking of a means of retaliation or escape, I just stood there, stunned. The figure started moving towards me at an unbelievable speed, and quickly, without thinking, my mind screamed, "Run!" I bolted as fast as I could down the street, but I was still a little drunk. I could hear him catching up to me and just before he finally did, I dropped to the ground and he tripped over me, completely unprepared for the accidental defensive strategy.

His hands couldn't react in time and he fell hard and fast square onto his chin. He squirmed a little on the ground and turned to face me. Blood was pouring out his chin like a faucet. It was pretty clear that he was badly injured, but he showed no signs of it. He must have been on some sort of amphetamine or speed, because he got up as if nothing had happened, wiping the blood away from his chin though it quickly reappeared.   By the time he stood up, I was also on my feet and had locked myself into a defensive position that I'd probably seen in a movie, though I was completely unprepared for that sort of thing. He leapt forward with a fist moving faster than his body and it struck me across the cheek before I could even think to react. The pain was unbelievable.

"Just take my wallet, man." I whimpered. "Just leave me alone."

"I don't want your fucking wallet!" He responded with another blow to my stomach. I felt like I was going to throw up, but instead it just sucked all the breath completely out of me. Punch after punch, face, stomach, my neck, I was being pummeled with no sign of escape. The blows stopped briefly and just as I was about to compose myself, he grabbed me around my neck with both hands and squeezed. Hard.   It took every ounce of energy to mumble out a "What do you want?" complete with coughs and grunts inserting spaces harshly between words.

He slammed my head against the brick wall of a store that had shut down hours ago. "I want you to stay away from Nicole. If I see you near her again, this might have to happen again, and next time I won't be so nice." As he said it, he spat violently onto my face. He was certainly not versed in hygiene, as he reeked of beer and days old sweat. He could have been one of the greatest bullies on TV. Just give this guy a job and maybe he won't be such a dick in real life, because he wouldn't want to take his work home with him.

That was certainly not how I pictured the rest of the evening going and I had no intention of making things worse. So I lied, "Ok. Just let me go. Please." He slammed me one more time against the wall and just before letting me go he kicked my feet out from under me so I fell on the sweat- and saliva-soaked sidewalk with enough force to make me cry out again in pain. "I'm serious." He added as he stumbled away, "Leave her alone. She's mine!"

It doesn't look like it to me, I wanted to scream back, but feared too much for my life. I realized then why Nicole was so shook up earlier. With this asshole in your life, how could anyone ever be happy? I sat there for a minute before attempting to get up. I had never been in a fight before, though I could have barely called this a fight (since that takes two), and decided then that I'd never really want to again. Some people were born to be warriors and I realized that night that I certainly wasn't one of them. I finally got myself to my feet like an old man and hobbled the rest of the way home.

Taking off my clothes, I saw cuts and the onset of bruises all over me. My eye told me that tomorrow it would dye itself black and blue in honor of the occasion. My lip decided that it wanted to be supportive and would stay cracked and bloody for a while and wondered if a rib or two wanted in as well. I started a bath full of hot water and stood looking in the mirror at the broken version of myself until the water was high enough to get into. This isn't right, I thought, as I stepped into the bath. I'd never taken a bath before in that tub and was as awkward with my body in it as a teenage lover fumbling and fidgeting about trying to be comfortable in his partner's naked skin. The only thing that seemed moderately comfortable was to lean back with my head resting on the edge of the tub and my knees poking out of the water like a sad pair of caged dorsal fins.

I let the water wash over my wounds as blood from my cuts turned the water a hazy pink. As I tried to relax, I let the whole scene play out again in my head, start to finish, without any commentary before going back to view it as a play by play with my inner cynic sportscaster. What the hell was this guy's problem? I certainly understood that if such a beautiful girl dumped you, it could be upsetting, but stalking her and assaulting any guy that she dates next is a bit extreme, even for someone slightly out of whack.

I debated calling Nicole to tell her what happened, but decided that no bad news should be given so late at night. At least let the rigors of the daytime mitigate the dark news. How could I expect her to get back to sleep after hearing that her ex had just assaulted me on my way home, probably after waiting for me the whole time I was at her apartment. But then I thought about her and the possibility of him deciding to head back to her place afterwards to wait for her. Maybe he wouldn't even wait. A sleepless night is way better than being harassed or assaulted by a madman.

Luckily, my phone was within my reach, nestled safely in the pocket of my pants. Nicole's phone, however, must have been sitting unnoticed while Nicole danced around getting ready for bed listening to a bold mix of songs I recommended. While the phone rang and rang, I pictured her undressing, dancing as if no one was watching, but as if I were there and it was my birthday or our anniversary or some other special occasion that warranted a moderately innocent striptease.

I didn't want to scare her so I decided to wait a few minutes before trying again. Nothing says be very scared than a collection of missed call reports from your phone in 30 second intervals. I closed my eyes and let my mind wander back to the thoughts of Nicole dancing around her room half naked. Just as she was about to finally get to the finale of her show, my phone rang and showed her face on its screen.

"Hey." I said with an odd blend of sexual intrigue and concern.   "Hey." She replied. "I was just getting ready for bed listening to some of those songs you gave me. They're all pretty great so far."

"Good I'm glad."

"What's up?" she asked knowing there was a reason for the out of turn call.

I sighed a pretty big sigh into the receiver before I finally got up the guts to say, "I ran into Mark on my way home."

"What do you mean? How would you even know who he is?"

"Well, he beat me up pretty bad."

"Oh my God, no."

"I'm ok now. I'll probably have a black eye in the morning, but shouldn't be anything that I can't handle."

"Oh Josh."

"I wasn't sure if I should tell you tonight because I didn't want you to worry, but he was hurt pretty bad himself and I had a thought that maybe he'd try to go back to your place. He was heading that direction when he finally let me go."

She didn't say anything.

"Nicole?"

After a couple beats she finally asked, "Josh, will you come back over?"

"Why? What do you think he'll do?"

"If you take a cab, you'd probably still beat him here."

"This was a while ago."

She didn't respond.

"Nicole, do me a favor and call the police, tell them about the restraining order and that you think he might be outside your house. I'll get in a cab and come right over, ok? That way we'll both hopefully be safe when I get there."

"Ok." There was no life in her voice anymore.

"Can you do that? Will you call the police?"

"Yeah, I can do that. I'll call right now."

"Don't go outside until they or I get there, ok?'

"Ok."

The water, stained with blood, marched slowly down the drain in formation. There are no amateurs here, I thought, as I looked up the number for a cab. Five minutes later the cab arrived like a B-52 picking up fresh soldiers to bring back to the front. I gave the address and we were off into the fray.

After walking around in the city, occasionally taking public transportation for so long, it was absurd how fast the cab got to her place at 3 in the morning. Maybe I did beat the old nut, I thought as I paid the cabbie off and walked out into the battle. I didn't see any sign of Mark and silently praised the gods for such luck. I rang up to her place and she let me in without hesitation.

I ran up the stairs to her door and before I even reached the entry, she flung herself on me as if I were a rock star and she was a groupie just waiting for the chance to touch me. Unfortunately, the pain and bruises made it hard to enjoy my moment of fame. It wasn't until we actually walked in the door that she noticed my confidently forming black eye and various cuts and bruises.

"Oh my God. I'm so sorry that you had to be a part of this." She spoke as if I were part of a Nazi work camp or something. "I'll be fine." I reassured her. "Really it's not so bad. A week or so and I should be back to normal." She poured me a drink and one for herself as well. As we sat on the sofa waiting for the cops to arrive, I recounted as best I could remember, the brawl that took place. It was an amazing sense of power I had as she oohed with every punch and winced with every mildly gory description of each blow. For the first time in my life I actually felt like a hero even though I had lost the battle completely.

Right during the final moments of the story, there was a buzz at the door. "Good, the police are here." Nicole sighed with relief. "Let me talk to them, ok? You just relax." And I did. I took a slug of whiskey, closed my eyes and felt it pass through my entire being like sweet, sweet love. The sound of Nicole screaming pulled me right back to reality. "No, Mark, get the fuck out of here, I don't want to see you anymore. The cops are on their way right now!...No... He's not here Mark...no I don't care what you saw.... please just leave me alone."

Two car doors slammed, silencing the argument and two sets of feet marched forward. I opened up a window to the front of the building to hear what was going on.

"Can I help you, sir?" a deep voice rustled.

"I'm just here to see my girl." A hesitant voice replied, apparently Mark's.

"What's your name?"

"Mark Dimble. What's yours?" Mark was trying to act tough now.

"Officer Lawrence."

"You bothering Ms. Narim again?"

"No, she asked me to come over." He lied as they shone a flashlight into his face.

"You ok?"

"Yeah I'm fine."

"You don't look so good. You in a fight?"

"Nah I just fell on my way over here." His confidence clearly waning.

"Let's say we take you to a hospital, eh?"

"Nah, I guess she's out for the night, I'll just head home."

"What do you say we take you home?"

"I'll just walk."

"We insist."

Mark started to run, the poor bastard, and tripped before he got to the end of the block. For a moment I almost felt sorry for him and his complete lack of common sense as the officer's footsteps slowed as they caught up to him. I could barely make out the words from that far away, but I did catch an echo or two of the prologue in the fabled 'you have the right to remain silent' act. I never imagined that I'd hear it in person. Nicole and I made our way downstairs to talk with Officer

Lawrence as Mark rested face down on the hood of the car mumbling obscenities to the system.

Mark's disobedient head was rammed into the backseat of the cruiser without any sense of patience or care. A quick wave and nod from the officer and he drove the mangy miscreant away. We stood there motionless for a minute until we could no longer see the difference between the night and the car, my arm wrapped casually around her shoulder as if I actually had the means to protect her from the world. It was clear, though, at least to me, that I was not a protector. The walk back inside to her apartment felt like we were running a marathon. Both of us completely drained from a truly ridiculous day. Our emotions were a stability ball trying to hold a small, very round woman on top of us.

Her bed welcomed us without any sense of lust or mischievous intent, but rather to hold our weary bodies and minds. Any prior thoughts of sexual intent we had when I was there earlier that evening were completely wiped clean from our minds and we fell asleep holding each other, fully clothed, waiting for a new day to come.

10

We woke up in the same position we fell asleep in. Despite the lack of sexual activity of the prior evening, our intertwined bodies made what seemed like a new Kama Sutra pose, completely by accident. I made a note of it for future reference. How someone looks at first light has always been important to me. It was a good indication of a person as a whole, especially when girls have the matters of make-up altering their true selves. I was happy to note that Nicole was a true beauty that morning. I hadn't thought about her not wearing any make-up the night before because everything was so intense. I realized now that I hadn't noticed her naked face.

The realization made me smile as she looked up at me from my chest, which she had used as a pillow. "What are you smiling about?"

"I just realized how beautiful you are without any make-up."

She glowed even more from the compliment.

"I'm so glad you came back last night," she whispered groggily, "I was so scared."

"Me too."

The pain in my body screamed at me as I made my first move to get out of bed and couldn't help but grunt a little. "Are you ok?" she asked.

"I'm just really sore."

I finally crawled my way out of bed and looked at myself in the nearby mirror for damage report. My eye was as black as I expected, my lips had multiple cuts, and I had a tattoo in the shape of Marks' hands circling my neck. I lifted up my shirt to reveal another batch of bruises on my stomach. For a second I actually felt like a bad ass, telling the story of my battles through the wounds on my body. Just as the story was about to get good, Nicole looked over and caught the tail end of it and ran over to me frantically.

"Oh my God," she cried, "that looks awful."

"It's really not so bad. I'm just sore."

"I'm so sorry, I'm so sorry," her fingers cried as she traced the bruises, nicks and cuts. When her hands roamed across my face I felt her shudder. I wrapped my arms slowly around her neck and pulled her into a hug. She tried to hide it, but her whimpers couldn't be hidden. Knowing she tried so hard to keep me from hearing her, I never said a word I just held her until she was ready to let go.

"Can I make you some breakfast?" she asked as she grabbed pans, a carton of eggs and some bacon and started cooking. I answered by sitting down at the table. "I have to go to class in a bit," she explained, "but feel free to hang out here until I get back. It's only an hour class." The smell of the bacon and eggs moistened my mouth and by the time she scooped some eggs from the pan I had already swallowed their weight in saliva. "There are towels in here if you want to take a shower and please just make yourself comfortable." A few more formalities and she ran out the door hoping to make it to class on time.

I ate way too quickly, as I tend to do, and wished I could have let the taste linger just a little bit longer. I cleaned up and washed the dishes that were in the sink. I felt like I had been driving all night so when I started to feel her lonely bed beckoning me back I gladly obliged. I didn't sleep, but I laid there staring around the room getting a backstage look at the life of Nicole. Not wanting to actually snoop around, I stayed in bed and just looked around. She didn't have a whole lot in her apartment, though I noticed an abundance of photos and photo albums. I hadn't had film developed in years and wondered how old the photos were.

Her laptop sat on her desk with the rest of her thick pile of overweight schoolbooks. Her computer's desktop picture was of her and another girl that I guessed was her sister and there was a surprising lack of icons on the screen. I would have guessed that she would be one of those people who tried to be organized, but their desktop got cluttered quickly from all the downloading and moving around of files. I was not one of those people and was pleased that she wasn't either.

A quick glance through her open closet doors showed bits of her sophisticated style. No slutty club clothes, no knee-high boots, just cute clothes that a young intellectual would wear, though nothing too conservative. I got up to go to the bathroom and on my way I glanced over at her laptop and noticed that she had received an instant message. Though I was trying not to snoop, I couldn't help but read it.

aligurll3: hey nicole, how'd it go last night?

It took me a minute to actually piece together the letters I was seeing into something that my brain could fathom. The last piece fell into place–that was Allison's screen name. *My* Allison. The very girl that denied me as a future part of her life and the girl that would be horribly devastated if she knew that at the other end of her innocent message stood the man who was betraying her. I tried to figure out how they might know each other, but I couldn't grasp at any ideas.

Allison went to BU and had graduated 6 years ago. They wouldn't have even been in college at the same time. She was from Vermont and Nicole was from Texas. They were almost exact opposites in every equation I popped them into. For a few minutes I thought of different scenarios in which they may have crossed paths and become friends, but my muse decided to call in sick and I kept coming up empty. Then the screen offered up another tease.

aligurll3: i still haven't heard much from my josh. i hope he doesn't stay too mad at me for long.

The feeling of momentary terror turned into a horrible dread that made my body weak and had to sit. Nicole told Allison about me. How could they not realize? I told Nicole everything about me and she probably relayed to her friend as anyone normally would. Allison had to have told Nicole about the proposal. Does Nicole know, but she doesn't want to let Allison know? The possibilities soared above my head like a squadron of fighter planes breaking the sound barrier. I covered my ears to try and dampen the sound, shaking my head wishing it would all go away.

A photo on her dresser pulled me away. Nicole was much younger in the photo, maybe 14 or 15, and she was just as beautiful. Around her were about 6 other girls about the same age with one older one in the middle. It was a little harder to see the resemblance, but I knew at once that she was none other than a younger Allison. My heart sank like a school bus. Summer camp. You have got to be kidding me. I could just see the scene...

After the hugs, laughs, goodbyes, and a few tears running down sun soaked cheeks, they exchanged information to keep in touch after camp was over. They of course would be the only two to actually stay in touch, until the era of automated social networking suddenly reunited everyone. Nicole must have looked up to Allison because she was many things that Nicole was not, but wanted to be. Allison must have liked Nicole for her kindness and curiosity. They had to have been instant friends from the first day of camp when Nicole's too large bathing suit top came off her as she dove into the river. Allison of course comforted her as the other girls laughed at her and her yet undeveloped body while her suit floated away down the river.

Further breaking my promise not to snoop, I shuffled through the rest of the shoebox full of camp photos finding so many pictures of them together that I wanted to vomit. The cuteness of seeing Nicole when she was younger was completely drowned in the lake at Camp Happenstance where my life was taking place. I also came across a few letters that Allison had written about how she got into BU and was so excited to be moving to Boston. I kept digging through and found one about me. Allison wrote about how she had met a guy named Josh and how she wasn't sure how she felt about him, but there was just something about him and that she'd give him a chance. It took a minute, but I was able to find the memory of how we met in my mental library.

Allison and I were both in school at Boston University in completely separate circles of friends. I hung out with the musicians who wished they were at Berklee and the writers who wished they were at Harvard. She hung out with the other physical therapists and pre-med students. We both lived in Warren Towers on the 17th floor high above Commonwealth Avenue. I had a few friends who were having a small party one night and everyone was hanging out with a few guitars, singing some random tunes. Allison lived on the opposite side of the hall, but one of her friends lived a few doors down from the party. They had stayed up late trying to study like good students and were having a hard time concentrating with our poorly played covers of classic songs bouncing around the hallway.

She got fed up with all the noise and came to tell us all to quiet down. Everyone at the party was way too cool to have some nerd tell them to shut up and so they didn't listen. In fact, everyone actually started to play and sing louder after she left. When the party started to die down, I knocked quietly on the girls' open door to see if they were still awake. "What?" came the answer from Megan, who lived in that room.

"I'm sorry to bother you guys, but I wanted to apologize for everyone else. It was pretty shitty of them to not quiet down a little."

Allison turned around in her chair to face the doorway. "Are you guys done now?"

"Yeah, everyone is wrapping things up."

"Good, maybe now we'll actually get some studying done."

She looked at me with so much hatred that I felt as if I had just been tossed against the lockers by a bully in grade school.

"Hey, so I was going to go downstairs to grab something to eat. Can I bring you guys some coffee or something as a peace offering?"

Megan happily accepted and Allison threw a "Fine" my way, which I caught over my shoulder like a wide receiver, before the door was shut. When I came back up, they were furiously memorizing various bones and muscles of the human body. I didn't say a word. Megan had left the door cracked and I just walked in, put two coffees on their desks and left. I decided that I'd just go back the next day and ask

Megan more about Allison. She couldn't always be that mean, I thought, and like a good waiter I was gone before they realized their coffees had arrived.

Nicole's shower was alien and didn't feel at all like mine. No two showers are ever the same and like a new lover, it would take some time to get used to the way they touched you. I let it get used to the feeling of washing over my body, hoping that eventually it would be as good at it as my shower was. I couldn't say how long I was in there, but it must have been a while because I heard Nicole shut the door behind her as she came in.

I turned off the water and dried off. I could hear Nicole clanging around in the apartment as she settled in. After quickly getting dressed, I walked out of the bathroom with a cleanliness that my mother would approve of. I was still a little damp as I walked out, but how could anyone get dry in a room full of steam? Nicole was sitting at her desk typing on her computer when she noticed me. "Hey, how was your shower?" I answered with a few casual words as I wondered if she was chatting with Allison online. Scenarios where I could sneak a peek at her computer without her noticing tiptoed through my brain as I tiptoed closer to her.

"How was class?"

"The usual. This class is always pretty dull. The teacher is a wench."

As she was telling me about her class, I was bending toward her pretending to dry off my hair, while looking inquisitively at the screen. I could barely make it out. There was one chat window open in the same place it was before. It was impossible to tell who the sender was from so far away. My eyes were good but not that good. Nicole responded to another message on her screen as she continued talking about her class. When she finished her story, she realized that I was behind standing her and swiveled her chair around immediately, blocking any view of the screen. I had accidentally positioned myself right next to the box of camp photos that my fingers were sniffing through earlier and she looked at me nervously before asking, "So, do you want to do something today?"

"Sure," I shrugged. "What did you have in mind?"

"I heard they're playing Bill & Ted's Bogus Journey as the midnight show at Fenway."

"Is that the first one or the second one?"

"I think it's the second one. Where they go to hell."

"Yeah alright, let's do that. I like that one."

For the first time in our short relationship, we both felt an awkward silence. She broke it with "Did you ever send that band your review of their show?"

"No, not yet. Let's do that now." I leapt over to her desk to catch a quick glimpse of her screen before she could change anything. For a split second before she closed the window I saw that it was Allison that she was talking to. Nicole pulled up the band's Myspace page. I shook my head unsure of what to do or say about the whole Allison thing. Clearly she doesn't want to tell me that she knows Allison. At this point, though, she was visibly nervous that I might know about it as well. I decided to let her be the one to bring it up.

"Here, you sign in and send them a message to go see your site." She directed me with a clack of her keyboard, like a film slate, to start the scene. I positioned myself in her seat and typed my email and password to log in. She leaned nervously over my shoulder watching my every keystroke, her eyes glued to the screen sloppily like a first-grader's art project. It was kind of cute how nervous she was, hiding her little secret. I debated how long to toy with her before revealing what was behind door numbered 'I already know.' I sent the band a message with a link to my blog saying that I really enjoyed the show and that I had written a blog about it. When I was done I leaned back in her chair and felt her relax for a moment.

"You mind if I check my email real quick?" I asked.

"Uh. Sure, go ahead."

I accidentally hit a keystroke combination that brought back up her iChat window and blinked my eyes in preparation for a quick glimpse of whatever they could take in. Eyes, don't fail me now, I thought, I don't often make you guys work hard. Do this for me. "Oops," I lied as she realized what was going on and grabbed my attention by spinning me around in the chair. "You know what we should do?" She tried to cover. "That band is playing again tonight just outside the city. You want to have an adventure?" The real question was whether or not *she* wanted the adventure. A surge of confidence lit a bright path from my brain to my lips as I apparently decided to call our little poker game. "When were you going to tell me that you know Allison?"

Her face went so white that if it weren't for the various imagery tacked up to her walls, she would have blended in. Her jaw dropped as if all her baggage had fallen from her overhead bin and was now dangling from her chin. I almost took joy in the fact that I had called her out so blatantly because I was normally on the other end of this game trying to clean up the debris from some wreck. "I didn't think you'd want to know about that," she said quite honestly.

"You didn't think that eventually it would come out somehow?"

"I guess I was just waiting for a time that seemed appropriate."

"When could that ever be appropriate?" I didn't want to sound like I was too angry about it, but apparently I was. The truest feelings come out when you don't think about them, when you just blurt them out while your inner censor is on a smoke break. She looked horrified and I realized that things weren't going as I wanted them to. "What have you told her about us?"

"I just told her that I met a great guy named Josh at a bar and we've been hanging out for a while. I really didn't go into much detail."

I looked at her as a teacher may look at a student he's disappointed with. He knows that the kid can do better and still has all the hope in the world for her to succeed, even though statistically she won't get any better because she didn't care enough. But she did care, I thought, and so I corrected myself. I shook my head for dramatic effect, waited a few seconds and then added, "When did you first realize that our Allisons were the same?"

"When you told me about how you proposed to her. Who else would have done the same? It had to be you that she always talked about." After a few seconds she finally asked, "How did you find out?"

I navigated back to the iChat window of her chat with Allison and scrolled up to the top. "This popped up as I walked by your desk on my way to the shower. I wasn't looking for it, but it grabbed my attention and I focused in passing on the name enough to recognize it." Then I pointed to the photos near the shoebox. "I swear I wasn't snooping around, but after that I saw this photo laying there."

"I thought that I had moved that box and cleared all those up after I figured out the connection, but I guess I just forgot." She smiled wryly for a moment before finally asking, "Are you mad?"

"How can I be mad? I can't be mad that you know someone that I know. It's just bizarre to me that you didn't tell me that you knew her. I'm not sure what that would have changed or anything, but it just seems like the right thing to do."

"I know. I just didn't know what to do."

"You can't tell her that it's me, though. You do know that, right? I haven't even told her that I've met someone else yet. If she found out, of course she'd be upset, but if it was with someone that she knew, that would be much worse."

"I wouldn't dream of it. She's going to hate me forever."

I hadn't thought about that part yet. She was absolutely right, though. Why would she even want to tell Allison? If they were at all close, that would have completely ruined their entire friendship. "Do you ever hang out with her?" I asked.

"Sometimes. When I first got here and started school, we hung out for a bit but lately we haven't seen each other much." After a moment's hesitation she continued, "Ever since you and I met, though, she's been wanting to hang out again."

"Now that she has more time on her hands and fewer companions..."

"Yeah, I guess."

"So what now?" I asked, with a hint of hope lacing the rough packaging.

"I guess one of us will eventually have to tell her, right?"

"Yeah."

"You should probably tell her."

"Honestly, before I found out about this, I wasn't going to tell her until I was confident that this was actually going to go somewhere."

"Oh." She was deeply hurt. Her body language signed the rest of the sentence for her: *you're not sure that it is?*

"Look, Nicole, it's been, what, 3 days? How can either of us be sure of anything? I mean I really like you a lot, but I was with her for 6 years and only a few days ago asked her to marry me. Do you know what I mean?"

Of course she did. She had just gotten out of a slightly abusive long-term relationship of her own and probably wasn't ready to make any of those decisions either. I saw the realization come to her gradually like an incoming tide—unless you pay close attention to it, you wouldn't see the transition from low tide to high tide, just the sudden rush of water against your feet out of nowhere.

"So what now?" she echoed my own question.

"That's the question of the hour, isn't it?"

"So how long were you going to wait before talking to her about it?"

"I didn't have a deadline for it, but it was certainly going to be a while."

"Don't you think she's curious what's going on?"

"Of course I do, but I'm bitter about her saying no to me and frankly I don't care. She can just stew in the pot she put herself into by saying no. It's her own fault as far as I'm concerned. She probably just thinks that I need some time and so I'm taking it."

"Actually, she's beginning to wonder about things."

"Oh?"

"She was asking my advice."

I waited for her to continue.

"She asked whether she should consider you lost or try to keep chasing you."

"What did you say?"

"Well, I told her that she needs to think about everything. She understands why you're so upset, but she still doesn't know if she's ready for all of that—marriage and kids and family life. I told her that if she's not ready, then maybe she should start letting go because that's what she'd have to accept if she stayed with you."

"How very wise you sound, but somehow very biased."

"What do you expect? I really want us to work out, Josh. I'm afraid of how fast everything inside me has been elevated with you. But here I am, with the doors opening up at the penthouse and my toes are just over the edge. I'm just hesitantly waiting in the elevator, far enough out to keep the doors open."

She seemed surprised by her own words and I complimented her analogy to myself, and I thought so did she.

"I know exactly how you feel," is all I could muster, unable to keep up with her wordplay.

"You should probably tell her something. Even if you just tell her that you need some space for a while. Not that you want to break up, but just that you need some time to think about things and that maybe she should think about things as well. That could give you at least a little bit of license to entertain the idea of meeting someone."

I nodded pensively, running scenarios in my head.

"Josh. My worry is that after some time apart she'll come running back to you wanting to get married. What would you do then?"

"I hadn't even entertained that idea yet. I honestly don't know." I realized that it was my turn to repeat the words of the day, "So what now?" We both relaxed a little bit despite all of the absurdity and smiled with each other. "What do you say we try and forget about questions for a while and just have some fun? I'll talk with her soon. Ok?"

"Ok." She answered with a shy smile as she sat on my lap draping her arms around me as if I were a hero come to slay her inner dragon. "I'm sorry you found out like this," she whispered into my ear, "but I'm glad that you know now."

"I still can't quite share your enthusiasm, but I'm glad that it leaves us without secrets so early on."

11

It was a beautiful afternoon and we decided to go for a walk around the city. I never spent much time on the Cambridge side of town and so we walked towards Harvard Square. Things seemed pretty much back to normal between us as we strolled our way through the streets. The unusual thing about new relationships is that they innately want to become grown-up relationships as fast as they can. They do this by pulling you to learn everything you can about each other, even though the most exciting part about a new relationship is the mystery of who the other person is. Part of me wanted to put a limit on how much we learned about each other day by day. That way maybe we could keep our new car smell for a little longer. Few people have that much self-control and neither of us could help it so we spent most of the day finding out as much as we could about each other.

I had always wanted to go to the Museum of Useful Things, right near Harvard Square, but Allison could have cared less, so we never did. Though it turns out it's less of a museum and more of a store. Either way, it was great to check it out. Of course we trespassed onto Harvard's precious lawns and read excerpts of novels out loud to each other as if we were students critiquing the great works of our generation with self-proclaimed authority. We walked around the grounds of the great school, toying with the idea of sneaking into a class to see what it was all about. At BU it would have been easy in most of the large classes. Anyone could have just waltzed right in, sat in the back and gotten the same education (sans degree, of course) for free. Neither of us had the guts to actually try it, so we had to pretend like we belonged as we roamed the grounds with our chins slightly higher in the air than we'd normally hold them.

At the aptly named store Joie de Vivre, we checked out and played with all sorts of trinkets. Everyone there seemed to love everything in the store, but no one seemed to buy anything. They had novelty items that had no real use in daily life. Toys from older generations lined the shelves like unwanted older dogs surrounded by puppies in a pet store. They were fun to look at and play with for a minute, but no one really wanted to take them home. Even the children we saw played with something for a minute and then let it go like Zen masters dumping their artwork in the river after spending a year crafting it. I wondered how such a place stayed open.

As our feet got tired from all the walking, our bellies tapped us from the inside reminding us what time it was, so we decided to grab a table at Grendel's Den before planning our next move. The conversation of a young couple at the table next to us was wafting over to us mixed with the clang of their bracelets and their hipster jargon—the Bayside Ramblers were having a secret show at the House of Blues.

"Josh, did you hear that? I love them. Can we go?"

"Who are they?" I was not in the know.

"Are you kidding? They're like the next big thing around here. Where have you been?"

Apparently not in college going out all the time, I thought, but only said "I don't know."

"You would love them. They have such a great show."

"Sure, let's check it out. Did the grapevine tell us what time?"

"No, but I'm guessing late if they're headlining."

"Alright, well let's run by after dinner, get tickets, and then we'll go from there."

"Perfect." She smiled and like every other time, it made me smile a little bit in return.

We both had cheeseburgers, which were unbelievable. The burger was so big that I felt like the waiter had set me down on my knees in front of a cow, tucked a bib into my shirt, and left me with an "Enjoy!" A real gourmet burger just can't be beat. By the time we had finished eating, the place had filled up with a clever mix of hipsters, smart but stupid coeds, and alcohol. Many good times would be had in this place, I imagined. As we paid our bill and walked out the door, I got a feeling of déja vu, but it was tugged away briskly by the chilly evening.

There was already a small line forming outside the House of Blues and as we walked up to it I got the stinging feeling of how much older I am than she. College kids look so young after you've been out for a few years. It's like going back to your old high school—though all the kids are exactly the same age you were, they still look like babies.

The ticket booth light had just flickered on. "Great, we're just in time." I smirked at the sight of the overly tattooed guy sitting behind the glass. He had an odd mix of a tough guy body and an emo-ish face and demeanor. I couldn't wrap my brain around what he was trying to be viewed as. "Can we get tickets for tonight's show?"

"Which one?"

"The one with The Bayside Ramblers," I said, turning to Nicole for visual confirmation.

"They're not playing tonight."

"Really? We got word that they're playing a secret show." My voice slowly turned more and more to a whisper leaning closer and closer to the glass with each word. Nicole, being the outspoken crafty one, had already taken a few people in for questioning and I caught the end of her first inquisition over my left shoulder.

Some slightly terrified young college guy gave her what she wanted to hear under the spellbinding bright heat of her eyes. "Say you're going to see The Last Resort. They're playing under a different name tonight because they're just testing out some of their new music on the crowd."

"Thanks." She bubbled and let her hand fall down from his shoulder, grazing the length of his arm on the way down. It always made me uncomfortable when I saw girls exploiting their sexuality to get what they wanted. It was probably just because I wished that I had the same power. I would have used such a gift at every possible opportunity. (*Sorry, crazy lady who orders stupid drinks at Starbucks, I didn't mean to spill that drink all over you. Please let me help you out. Come in the back and we'll get you cleaned up.*) I shouldn't have gotten jealous, because I knew what Nicole was doing, yet the feeling grabbed onto my ankles and sat on my feet like an annoying young cousin.

"Right, then. We'll take two tickets to go see The Last Resort." As he swiped my card I decided to throw it in his face a bit. "You know, you could have just told me that they're playing under a different name when clearly that's who we wanted to see."

"I'm not supposed to tell people that information so that we can keep people like you out."

"People like me?"

"We try to keep a certain type of clientele."

I looked over my shoulder and back at the guy behind the glass. "Oh, so college kids and queers?"

"Josh!" Nicole was appalled.

"You're right, sorry—*homos*," I said as I pointed my thumb in his direction. He wanted to break through the glass. "Whoa, there tiger." I continued. "I doubt you want to start attacking customers. That never looks good for a business."

He composed himself and slid the tickets underneath the window, trying to do it with as much force as you can, but that's like drinking from a straw—no one ever looks tough doing it. "Thanks!" I said cheerily as I snatched the tickets.

"What was that all about?" Nicole was clearly thrown off.

"He was giving me shit and I'm not in the mood for it." She curled the corner of her lip into an upside down smirk in disappointment.

"Hey, I'm sorry, alright?" Oh god, I've lost her for the rest of the night, I thought. Although guys don't have the sexual persuasion techniques that women do, we do have the ability to shrug off a lot of frustration and anger. Women tend to hold it in like a long bong hit of laced with PCP. They spend the rest of the night unaware of their own strength, ruining the night for everyone around within a half-mile radius. I had to get her to cough it out before too much of it entered her brain.

"I am so excited!" I tried hard to sound convincing.

"But you don't even know them."

"Well, aren't you glad that you'll be able to witness the moment when I realize their greatness? See my face drop?" The corner of her mouth flattened. I was on my way.

"Hopefully all these new experimental songs are as good as the ones that I know." Her tone teetered with one foot in excitement and the other in anger.

"I'm sure they're amazing. Aren't you excited that you'll get to be the first of all your friends to hear them? When the new album finally comes out, you'll be able to say that you were the first to see them all performed live. Maybe I'll write a review about it."

"I think you should."

We made our way to the end of the line, which would grow exponentially as show time grew closer. I wondered how everyone who knows the band got word of the show. Did the band advertise it on their site? If they were that new, did they really need to go out under a different name? Apparently they did. By the time the doors opened, they were sold out and turning people away. I wondered what their regular shows were like if their fake shows drew this much of a crowd. We were herded quickly into the club like cows to the barn. The herd stopped moving as the first few hit the stage and sent a traffic ripple all the way to the back, which is where we would stand for the remainder of the evening.

I looked around the room filled with young faces and wondered when I stopped being a member of this cool kid club. Is your membership card revoked the day you graduate from college or do they wean you into adulthood with a few year grace period? The club's stereo blasted some punk band as everyone waited for the show to start.

"You want a drink?" I yelled over bass that was thick and angry enough to kick a puppy.

She nodded "Yes," amplifying her rhythmic head bob to the music. At the bar I ordered us our 'usual' drinks and turned to look around at the crowd. I still had that awful feeling of being old, but had shaken some of it off when I noticed that many of them couldn't order drinks. Suckers! A feeling of fear grabbed the corner of my eye with a hook and forced my head to turn towards the door. I couldn't help but turn and my knees nearly buckled. *Allison*. What was she doing here? She was never in this part of town. I turned quickly back to face the bartender as he finished making the drinks. I hurriedly gave him some cash, told him to keep the change, grabbed the drinks and scurried back to Nicole.

I could feel the fear in my skin like a leech slowly sucking what little confidence I had left. Nicole noticed the look of terror on my face. "What's wrong? Was the bartender a ghost?"

"I think I saw Allison walk in." I yelled as I placed her whiskey sour into her grip.

"Are you sure?"

"I'm pretty sure."

"Did you talk to her yet?"

"When would I have talked to her?"

"I don't know!"

The wheels were turning in her head.

"Well I guess we'll just have to finally talk to her, won't we?"

"Somehow I doubt this is a good place to talk." I yelled extra loud to exhibit my point.

"Well what do you want to do? You want to stand in separate places?"

I let the weight of my head fall onto the back of my neck. "I don't know. This is dumb."

The lights went dark and the place erupted into applause as the opening band strolled onto the stage taking their places and grabbing their instruments. I didn't expect much out of these guys, but my mood was directing my thoughts at this point and it was not to be trusted. There should be a rule about judging things when you're in a foul mood. It shouldn't count. (Of course you hated my movie, your dog just died!)

After their short set, there was an even shorter break for the next band to go up. As the lights brightened a bit, I ducked my head down hoping not to be noticed by anyone that wasn't supposed to see me. I felt like a fugitive and like Harrison Ford standing in a watery tunnel, I was ready to jump. The next band was slightly better, but I couldn't actually make any reasonable judgements.

By the time The Bayside Ramblers, I mean The Last Resort, came on I was so terrified that Allison had surely spotted me that I couldn't enjoy myself. I envisioned her standing in the balcony, watching me as Nicole grabbed my hand with both of hers and kissed me on the cheek before telling me when her favorite song came on. I tried not to think about it. Allison was probably way in the back and there was no way she could see either of us. I tried to think about how she would have known about this show. I was always the one that suggested new music. She really didn't even listen to much music other than what I put on. She never rocked out to her ipod or played music when we slept together. She never suggested going out to shows or even sang in the shower. I peeked over to Nicole and was surprised that her lip had once again been curled in an upwards position.

Halfway through their set, my mind was so exhausted from worry and fear that it finally relaxed if only out of necessity. The band really was amazing. They looked good together, as any good band should. They each had their role and played it perfectly like a well-acted theater. The drummer was solid and though he wasn't flashy, he definitely surprised us and himself a few times. The bass player moved only as much as his role required and concentrated mostly on his backup vocals, which were soaring, so his lack of motion never bothered me. The lead guitar player wasn't too much of a diva and only stepped out and cranked his volume when it was clearly his turn, then he tucked himself back into the mold of the band and blended right back in. The singer/rhythm guitar player was the perfect front man. He had the coolest haircut, the tightest pants and had the attention of every girl there. He was probably the main reason for Nicole's enjoyment of the band along with every other coed in town.

After playing their last number, the band introduced the members (though clearly everyone knew them) and thanked the crowd for seeing the show. The lights went back up and everyone lingered until they were herded back outside to once again graze the streets. I watched the door vigilantly, looking to confirm my sighting. Finally I saw Allison's light brown hair (though it was cut shorter than it was a few days ago) twirl as she looked to her left, smiling. I had forgotten how beautiful she was. It's amazing how, after seeing the same face for a while, it becomes so much a part of you that you don't see it as everyone else does. I followed her gaze and to her left saw a dark-haired European looking fellow walking beside then moving behind her to the exit line. He followed her closely as she walked, tracing her footsteps with his feet.

It didn't occur to me right away that she could be on a date. It took a minute, after they were out the door, that the realization hit me. I turned to Nicole. "It *was* her." I said in amazement. "I saw her walk out."

"Are you ok?"

"I think she was with a guy."

She raised an eyebrow.

"You think she was on a date?" I continued.

"Maybe. You are."

I didn't know what to say.

"What, are you jealous or something?"

"I think I might be a little bit."

"How can you be jealous of her going out on a date when you are too?"

"I don't know how feelings work. I just feel them."

She flashed her lips, pursed out like a duckbill in frustration. "I guess I just didn't expect she'd start dating again so quickly."

"Once again, you did."

"Yeah but I was the one that was rejected." It somehow made sense in my head.

"Come on, let's go."

And just like that, the corner of her lip was once again turned downward and I let out a sigh for letting her slip back into the dark side.

We were one of the last people to walk out into the cold. A group of girls and their reluctant, jealous boyfriends were waiting around for the chance to try and meet the band. Another huddled group was smoking and I guessed that most of them were Berklee kids by the way they were judging the band's performance. It's hard to enjoy a show when you're being critical of every member's musical performance. I was glad that I had decided not to go to music school. I would probably have ended up liking music, especially live music, a whole lot less.

Nicole slid her arm through mine as I tucked my hands as deeply into my barely warm pockets as they could go. Just as she locked herself onto my arm, she suddenly stopped, jerking me backwards. "What are you...?" Her face went bright red, then turned pale, like a sun suddenly transitioning from red giant to white dwarf, ready to explode and die out completely. I found my footing again and looked up, following Nicole's line of sight from her eyes in slow motion, like in a horror movie. I expected to see Freddy Kruger standing there waiting to kill with his metal claws and messed up face. Instead I saw Allison, staring blankly back at me.

"Hi." She said wryly.

"Hi." I hit the ball back to her court.

"Great show, neh?"

"Um. Yeah."

"Hey, I'm Sascha." The mystery man identified himself, holding out his hand pleasantly.

"Josh." I put my hand out for him to grab and shake. I expected him to say something like 'Oh, you're Josh. I've heard all about you.' or something stupid like that, trying to be cordial. But he really just hadn't heard of me. He had no idea.

"I met Sascha the other day after going to Shaw's. My bags buckled and my stuff fell all over Marlborough Street. He helped me carry all my food home." Allison explained.

"Isn't that nice." I tried to sound as sincere and unknowing as I could. "Well isn't she lucky that you were there to rescue her."

Allison was staring Nicole down so hard that I thought Nicole's skin might bruise, and I thought I saw her wince in pain.

"I'm Nicole." She said hesitantly, sticking out her hand to Sascha before making her way over to her old friend turned sudden enemy.

"A pleasure." Allison squeezed out tightly, completely devoid of cordiality.

The air was so tense that for a moment I thought "Poor Sascha," when really I had no sympathy for him whatsoever. The tension, thick like fog, made it difficult to breathe or speak, but somehow I decided to throw it out there. "I met Nicole the other night at Our House."

"How wonderful." Alison lied.

"I love that place. I especially love that bartender who always wears that same shirt with the bolo. He's funny." Sascha tried to chime in.

This guy really doesn't get it, does he? Maybe he just really doesn't want to have this ruin his evening. He must have finally caught on to the general intensity of the moment and retreated back into his own mouth to defend his fort. I don't think anyone knew what to do next. I was angry at Allison for going out with this guy. Allison was angry at me for being out with Nicole. Nicole was upset that Allison probably hated her now as well. And Sascha, well, who cared about him at that moment other than himself?

Should we talk about things more? I thought, but ultimately concluded that this was clearly not the time or place to have any serious discussion. It has been my experience that discussions when any member of a party is angry are completely worthless and they never lead to a positive finale. It was better to wait for everyone's food to cool down before starting to eat, otherwise someone would walk away with a burnt tongue. I hate having my tongue burnt, so I finally decided to take the next step. "Well, it was great to see you Allison and to meet you, Sascha. You two have a great night." I was a true gentleman pulling out chairs and opening doors with my top hat and monocle squinched to my eye.

Relief, like a fairy godmother, came around to each of us and tapped our heads with her glowing wand with a star on the end, awakening us from our trances. A few final pleasantries and we started our long journey home. I could hear Sascha trying to dig into Allison with an old, dull pickaxe looking for some kind of explanation of what the hell that was all about. Knowing Allison, he wouldn't find any gold for years and would eventually either die or give up and head back east.

Neither Nicole nor I spoke for a few minutes until we were well away, far enough from Sascha's dig site. She eventually broke the silence with a hammer. "She hates me."

"I think she hates me more."

"Yeah."

A moment more of silence.

"We were better friends than you probably realize." She continued.

"I saw all the photos."

"That was like 6 years ago. We've stayed in touch ever since then. I basically came to Boston so that we could be closer."

"I still can't believe you didn't tell me sooner when you realized that it was her I was talking about."

"What would you have done? Would you have said that we shouldn't see each other anymore?"

"I don't know what I would have done, but it just would have been good to know."

"So now what?"

"I have to go talk to her."

"Should I talk to her?"

"Not yet."

I wanted to put my arm around her as we walked, but it felt like Allison could still see us and I didn't want to make things worse. Is this how it's going to feel from now on, like she's always watching me? I was feeling guilty enough before, but now?...But now she's dating someone, so how can she be mad that I am too? It struck me, "Did you know about that guy?"

"She told me that she was going out with him tonight, but she didn't say where."

"That's what you were chatting with her online about, wasn't it?"

"Yeah."

I shook my head. It was all so stupid. Really I had no right to be angry, but I was. I wasn't used to having that amount of the feeling inside me and my body wasn't sure how to cope with it. 'Who's this new kid in town?' my cells asked as my blood temperature rose.

"Josh, I'm sorry. I know this must be hard for you."

That was an unusual thing to say, I thought. As she realized what can of worms she may have accidentally opened, it made me wonder out loud: "Did she really just meet him?" I asked. Nicole's face answered for her, looking tired from all the emotional strain it had to withstand all night. Again I shook my head. "How long?"

"A few weeks or so."

"Is he why she said no to me?"

"He was probably part of it."

The anger inside started a reign of terror over my body—a coup of unimaginable tyranny, I found myself unable to control my motor functions. I just wanted to scream. That prick was the reason all of this happened?! Mr. Nice Guy with the $100 haircut and $300 shoes. Nicole was rubbing my arm though I couldn't feel anything except pain and anger. I looked at her and saw her sifting through words and rearranging them in her head, like a magnetic word jumble on the fridge, trying to find the right combination that would make things right.

"Let's go somewhere and get a drink."

"I think I'd rather drink at home. I'm not in the mood for people, loud music and yelling."

"You can come over to my place if you want, unless you want to be alone."

"I'll decide when we get to your place."

"Ok. Josh. I just want to help. I know this is hard for you, but I want to be here for you. The whole thing hurts me too."

"I know."

"Let's just take a cab. It's cold."

"I want to walk."

"Ok." Her grip on my arm tightened trying to absorb some of the heat emanating from the oven within my skin.

We walked the mile or so back to her apartment and I decided for some reason to come up. I definitely wanted a drink, and thought I wanted to avoid people in general. I didn't really want to drink alone, so Nicole was the best bet. She poured us some drinks and handed me mine after I slumped onto her sofa and kicked my shoes off pushing the heels with my toes. I took a sip, leaned my head back and closed my eyes. "Can we put on some quiet music or something?"

"Sure what do you want to hear?"

"Do you have Kid A?"

"Of course I do."

It was rare for anyone, especially for a group of people, to just sit and listen to music anymore. Sure it was always in the background at parties, but no one actually listened to it. Instead they just yelled over the top of it to hear each other, making everyone else yell louder in turn. I didn't feel like yelling or really even talking and hoped that Nicole could sense that somehow. As she slouched right next to me on the couch, I wondered what our dynamic was going to be. *Everything, in it's right place*, Thom Yorke whispered as she rested her head on my shoulder. We sat there for the duration of the album just listening and thinking to ourselves. I mulled around through my own garden of doubts, trying to find any weeds to pluck out, while Nicole was off somewhere I didn't know, probably trying to make sense of her own relationship with Allison.

At first, all I could find inside was anger. Anger at Allison for moving on so quickly, anger at Nicole for being so close with me and not telling me. Anger at happenstance for its absurd timing. Anger at myself for being so angry. I hated being angry and every time I got this angry it made me more angry at the fact that I was so angry. I realized though that I couldn't really be mad at any of those things. The cacophonous ending of "The National Anthem" pulled all the anger out from under my feet and I fell back.

I felt an odd calm come into me, through the top of my head right as "How to Disappear Completely" made its entrance. I was always of the mindset that whatever will be, will be. We can only just try to control our own lives, that because our lives are so hopelessly entangled in the choices of others, we can never have full control over our destiny or fate or purpose or whatever you want to call it. The choices we make define us, of course, but so do the choices of everyone around us whether we know them or not. Instead of contemplating what-if scenarios, I always just tried to accept things.

Why shouldn't Allison have gone out with some guy? He seemed like a nice guy, a tool, but a nice guy. I hadn't talked to her in almost a week and she was pretty convinced that I wasn't going back. Who can blame her? Granted, he was the reason she didn't want to stay with me, but then again I had my own doubts about everything between us. He could have just rescued me from a life that I wouldn't want in the end. Maybe everyone would be happier this way after all. There is always the possibility of a better life with every change that we face, but sometimes we have to look hard for it. I read a book once that asked me to write out a list of every bad thing that had happened to me and then write all the good things that came out of each bad thing. There were always at least a few. Sometimes they were things that changed my life completely. For the better.

Apparently I had fallen asleep in the garden I was tending in my head and had been gone for a while. With my epiphany that everything was probably pretty ok, the album had finished and the apartment rested silently. Nicole had fallen asleep. In a mirror across the room, I could see her face reflected. She truly was beautiful and for a few moments I studied her face as an artist might, preparing for a portrait. For a second, I wished that I could draw or paint so that I could capture her the way I saw her. Then I thought that even if I wanted to, I could never get her just right and would feel terrible that I ruined such a beautiful face. I used to feel that way about Allison too and realized that I was beginning to have a skewed perspective on love. When you believe that life is ever-evolving, it's hard to imagine yourself with one person, and I wondered how long this feeling with Nicole would last before one of us moved on.

I shook the feeling off like a wet dog and thought that it would be silly to go through life with that attitude. Even if that were the case, we should still be able to enjoy each other for the time that we have together. As lightly as I could, I moved Nicole's head from resting on me to resting on the back of the sofa. After another good look at her, I leaned in and kissed her. She woke up, slightly startled at first, jerking a bit out of her sleep, but then settled back into a relaxed position and wrapped her fingers around the back of my neck, tousling my hair. My hands roamed over her body as if I were cautiously driving in a new city, unsure of the streets. She reached down and grabbed my shirt with both hands, pulling it above my head.

Slowly we made our journey over to her bed, leaving a trail of our clothes behind us like a twisted adult version of Hansel and Gretel.

12

When I woke up the next morning, for the first time in a long time, I actually felt refreshed as if I had been hibernating with the bears all winter. Nicole was asleep, still naked, and thanks to some well-placed sheets her whole body looked laid out like a fine Renoir. I was hoping she wouldn't wake up for a few minutes just so I could take all of her in for a while longer. Right as the thought came to my head she opened her eyes and pulled the sheets up over herself—not out of shame, but out of necessity. It was a chilly Boston morning. She snuggled up next to me and put her head on my chest dragging her fingertips across and around my stomach.

"How are you feeling this morning?" she whispered.

"I feel wonderful. You?"

"Me too."

"Last night was just what I needed." Realizing how that might sound, I decided to explain further. "I love that we just sat there listening to music in our own worlds of thought. I don't think people do that anymore. I love that we did."

"Me too. I'm so glad you decided to stay," she said, taking a deep breath. I imagined that she was recounting the whole night's experience. I ran my hands around the small of her back as she moved her fingers around my body. She had the softest touch and I tried hard to mimic her performance. She turned slightly to face me and kissed me. If the next scene were in a movie, the camera would have drawn backwards and out the window to keep things at a PG-13 rating.

She jumped into the shower and I decided to make us some breakfast. I found a few eggs in the fridge and started up the oven. Cracking the eggs on the edge of the pan to a loud sizzle, I let my mind wander to Nicole in the shower. I smiled to myself when I realized that this time I didn't have to try so hard to picture her naked in the shower. I didn't know how she liked her eggs, but the last time she made me eggs they were scrambled so I decided that was the best bet. I wondered though if she was just trying to make what she thought I'd like. Eventually we'd find out the way each other liked their eggs and we wouldn't have to wonder, but for the time being it was fun guessing. And besides, neither of us cared if the other was wrong, we were just glad to be around each other. That's how things should always be, I thought.

Just as the eggs were getting done, the sound of the shower stopped. Perfect timing. She walked out of the bathroom wrapped in a towel, her hair still dark and wet. Girls never look as good as they do when they get out of the shower, at least the ones that don't need a great deal of makeup. I smiled as I looked up at her. Feeling self-conscious after a moment, she asked "What?"

"I'm just looking at you," I answered quietly. "Breakfast is almost ready."

I wondered for a moment what it would be like to say that to her every day, but quickly brushed the thought off. It was way too early to think about that sort of thing. She must have thought she was out of my view as she was getting dressed, but her strategically placed mirrors allowed me to watch her. It's amazing how different people act when they think no one is watching, even if they're in the same room. I can't say that she did anything unusual or weird while getting dressed, just that I felt like she did things a little bit differently, with a little less elegance.

Presentation has been proven to be important for just about any aspect of life and I had hoped to create a great ambiance, but with eggs, toast and little else it was hard to create a mood. "I love the smell of eggs in the morning," she said as if she knew that I was waiting for a confirmation. "Thank you," she added as she kissed me lightly. "I have class for most of today, but you're more than welcome to come over tonight. I'll have to do some studying for a big test that I have tomorrow, but other than that I'm yours."

"I need to find myself some work. I was thinking about trying to write a review of the show last night. Though I'll have to try and not write it as if I knew Allison was there the whole time."

"I think you should. I love that we have a reason to go see shows now. Did you ever hear back from the Wally and the Whale?"

"I haven't looked at a computer since yesterday. I guess I'll find out when I head home."

"Well, now that I have nothing to hide on my computer, you're welcome to use this one." She said it unsure of how I would take it, but as it turned out we were both ready to laugh about it. And we did. After what we both went through the night before it was hard to still be upset at each other.

"Well, thanks, but I'll probably head home, whenever you have to leave, and get started trying to really sort my life out."

"That sounds like a good plan." She was genuinely happy and for the first time in a while, so was I. As we finished our eggs and toast, her curiosity begged her to ask, "Josh, I'm just curious. What did you do with the ring that you bought for Allison?"

"Why, do you want it?" Even though it was a joke it was a dumb thing to say, so I quickly followed with a normal answer. "I still have it in my apartment somewhere. I suppose I'll return it soon. I'll certainly need the money since I haven't found a damn job yet. At this point, I'd be fine with taking any stupid job just to make some money until I find something that was right for me. It's ironic that I worked extra hard and saved as much as I could for that ring and now it'll be the very thing that gets me through my unemployment."

"We'll find you something."

With that, we got ready and walked out the door to face our day. Later, as I thought about the ring, I realized that I wasn't exactly sure where I put it, so I left myself a mental Post-it to remember to grab it and return it later that day.

☂

"Let me know if you're coming over later on, ok?"
"Of course. Have a good day."
"You too."

The simplicity of our conversation was the important part. There wasn't any crap, just life and we were living it. She kissed me lightly before she changed her course en route to the campus. I kept walking up and over the bridge back to Back Bay and back to my own apartment. Because it was only slightly out of the way I decided to stop into Sweet & Nasty to see what the word was there. Through the window, I could tell that Carrie was clearly having a hard time getting through the day. "Hey," I said as I made my way through the door, "what's going on?"

"Oh, you know."

"No, actually I don't. Maybe if I had a job here, I would. But I don't."

She shook her head and smiled. "What are the chances that she was the one that you spilled that coffee on?"

"About 1,000,834 to 1." I said explaining that statistics was an odd hobby of mine.

"Right. Well, I doubt you'll get the job. You seem like an interesting guy, but there's no way that she's getting past whatever it is that you did or didn't do to her."

"I know. I was just stopping in on my way home."

"Well Karen is actually expected in at some point soon so you may not want to be here."

"What else can she do to me, right?"

"Ha," She laughed awkwardly as if she didn't know if she should or shouldn't. "I suppose you're right."

"Have you guys found anyone for the job yet?"

"No, that's actually why I'm a little flustered. I'm supposed to have the next few days off, but because no one can cover for me, I can't."

"That's a drag." What can you say in a scenario like that?

We stood there in awkward silence as we both looked around at the phallus-shaped candies and the extensive collection of vibrators and dildos.

"Well," I broke the silence, "I guess I'll get going."

"Alright. I'll remind Karen that you're still interested, but like I said..."

"I don't have a chance, I know. It's OK."

"Take it easy."

"Will do."

As I made my way out I noticed Karen walking toward the store and debated whether or not to say anything. She was on the phone and couldn't be bothered to see the cars that almost killed her as she crossed the street, so I figured that whatever I said would just float away in the breeze to another set of ears that wouldn't care what they were hearing. I decided to ignore her and head home, so I and crossed the street before she would have been in range to notice me.

I ran up my steps and into my apartment that for whatever reason suddenly seemed like a shit hole. It wasn't until after I graduated and started living on my own that I realized the dorms I lived in all through college would be far better than any apartment I could actually afford. Especially now, with no job.

As usual, the first thing I did was take a shower in the shower that knew and loved me. But this time, it didn't quite feel right. I just kept thinking about Nicole and envisioning her in her shower and how she looked when she walked out of the bathroom wrapped in a towel. Unfortunately Allison popped into my head soon thereafter and ruined the whole fantasy. I started wondering if she had slept with Sascha yet. It's amazing how territorial people can be considering that statistically they're going to be with someone else eventually, and so am I. In fact, I am with someone else, but it still upset me to think of Allison with someone else. Now that I was with Nicole, though, the feeling was probably more diluted than if I hadn't been.

Eventually I let thoughts of Allison flow down the drain with the rest of the dirt, sweat, anger, frustration and love from the night before, and I stepped out onto the cold tile. Much like my own mind, my computer never slept and was waiting to tell me all sorts of things that I had missed. I sorted my way through the junk mail and found the few messages that I'd actually want to read. One of them was from Allison. She never wrote me emails, so I knew that it had to be something awful. I decided against reading the 9-paragraph email for now. I'll get to evaluating that dissertation later, I thought, and kept browsing. Signing onto Myspace, I noticed that a new message from Wally and the Whale had been dropped into my in box. Apparently they loved my review and were glad to have someone who was so attuned to music at their show. Of course they loved my review. All I did was praise them. They also mentioned that they had a new album coming out and would love to have me review it if I wanted to. Of course I asked them to mail me a CD and that I'd be glad to.

I took a shot of confidence from someone liking my writing, no matter how trivial it was, and with a slight buzz I was ready to keep going with it. I tried to remember the show from the night before without Allison in it. It was surprisingly hard to do considering that for the last few days I hadn't thought of her more than once or twice a day, if that. In my false memories of the previous night, Allison was always watching me, judging me. She never took her eyes off of me the whole time and it was making me absurdly uncomfortable. I couldn't concentrate on the memory of the band's performance because she just stood there watching me. If you imagine what it might feel like to have someone watching you as you pee, it's probably the same feeling. You want to go, you have to go, but you just can't with someone watching you like that. Something had to be done to shake this. I decided to face her. I was David and she was the Goliath of my thoughts. She had to be taken down. There was only one problem; she was going to be at work all day.

I toyed with the idea of going to talk to her at her office, but quickly decided against that for obvious reasons. I would just have to wait until she got home from work. With that, I decided to take a trip to Freedman Jewelers downtown and return the ring that I worked so hard to buy. I opened up my top desk drawer, where I kept all the other things that ended up being useless, and shuffled though some things. It wasn't there. I tried the next drawer, but found nothing but papers and random receipts. The third drawer never had anything to offer, but I looked in anyway. I was getting frantic. No, I thought, you can't lose the ring. How could you lose the ring? I looked around my desk, the floor. Nothing. I looked in the kitchen through every drawer. Nothing.

I'd lost my keys before, I had even lost a huge report in college that I had to turn in minutes later, but I had never had such a feeling of loss in my life. It was so terrible that for a moment I considered going back to my long–abandoned Christian faith and pray to St. Christopher, hoping that he'd embrace me once again as his child and help me. It's amazing how people turn to faith when they need something. If I was going to pray, I might as well have asked the Boogie Man to help me, but of course that just sounded silly.

I ran through possible locations of where the ring might be systematically, tracing its whereabouts. Clearly I had it at the carnival. I know I put it back in my pocket at the carnival. After we left, we went back to her place. I know I had it when we got there because I put it on the nightstand. On *her nightstand*. It had to still be at Allison's and I cringed. I suddenly had another reason to go pay her a visit. This is going to be a fun day, I thought.

I had to get out and do something. Anything. If I sat in my apartment all day I would go crazy. A walk turned out to be the best choice. I grabbed my ipod on the way out and cued up something that would agree with my mood. The band Blindside. Perfect. I decided to head down Commonwealth Avenue and skip the pompous air of Newbury. I wasn't in the mood for chic or hip. I just wanted to be alone for a while. If you've never walked down Commonwealth Ave then you're missing out. It's a magical street.

I made it all the way through the Commons, passing the duck pond with the paddleboats, hippies, college kids, and tourists. I decided to sit on a bench and rest for a moment. After a minute or two a group of ducks caught my attention. There was a larger duck, probably the father, with about eight little ducklings following him. At first I thought the adult duck might be the mother, but it didn't seem to have the caring nature that mothers normally have. He walked with a bit too much force to be feminine. The eight chicks walked in a straight line formation behind him, almost as if they were marching. Maybe he's not the dad after all, I thought. Maybe they were all sent to military school and he was their drill sergeant marching them across the parade grounds.

As they were passing right in front of me, he must have called "Halt" because they all stopped moving. The dad turned around and quacked a bit at the little ones. I didn't know what he was saying just yet, but I later realized that he must have said, "Do not go into the water without me." I know he said this because two of the smaller ones at the back of the line chirped quietly, daring each other to jump in. When the rest of them started marching forward again behind their dad, the two at the back stayed behind and walked up to the edge of the pond. There's a slight drop of about 6 inches from ground to water without a slope whatsoever. To a little duck it must be like looking over the edge of the Cliffs of Dover. The one proposing the dare was clearly antagonizing the other. The dared one stepped back and forth, shaking his tiny wings, trying to decide the severity of the situation.

After what seemed like the other one chanting, "Jump. Jump. Jump." the little guy jumped and plopped without a sound into the pond. They both laughed for a moment until the realization came that he couldn't get out. He swam back and forth awkwardly at the edge of the pond looking for some sort of a slope to walk back out on. After a few seconds he started screaming in terror. He must have been saying, "Dad, Dad, help!"

The rest of the group halted again at the dad's command and he turned his head around to see one of the stray chicks at the edge of the land looking down into the water. The dad didn't rush, but he turned around and very orderly made his way back to the rebels. The rest of the chicks chatted back and forth falling out of formation.

The dad peered over the edge and saw the little one flailing in the water trying to find a way out. He quacked once or twice, probably saying "I told you not to go in without me." He made no attempt to save the little one. He'd have to figure it out on his own. After scolding the one who dared the other to jump in, he gathered everyone back together and they left. The little one in the water was frantic, probably looking about the same as some other species watching me as I looked for the ring.

The formation of ducks walked away and the littlest one could eventually see them as they neared the edge further down the bank. He swam as fast as his little legs could go and found one of the few slopes down into the pond. He wasn't welcomed back into the group with a victorious cheer, he just got back in line at the back and went on with what turned out to be a swimming lesson.

Watching the whole thing unfold was enlightening. The dad wasn't being mean, he was just teaching his son a lesson—do what I tell you to do. He knew that eventually the little one would find them where he was taking them all. A sub-lesson was that there's always an answer to a problem. You can always figure out an answer, little one. It was a lesson that all of them would have to learn and so would I. Thanking them silently from afar, I decided to head home. Thanks to the ducks I was ready to put the angry music to bed and put on something a little more playful for the walk home.

With an oddly renewed sense of vitality and literally a bird's eye view of my life I walked home and started writing about the show from the night before. It came to me like a dream and was gone just the same. When I finished, I posted it, sent them a message on Myspace and hoped that I'd hear back.

The all too familiar walk to Allison's was darkened by the ominous clouds hanging over both our lives. I felt a surprising calm as I rang her buzzer. I had thought to use my key knowing full well that it would probably be the last time I'd be able to use it, but decided that would be pretty rude, even for me. When the door finally opened, I wasn't greeted by Allison, but rather by her evil twin who clearly had no intention of playing nice.

"Hey." I said.

"Hey." She echoed slightly distorting my pleasant tone.

"So I think we need to talk about some things."

"You think?"

"Well, can I come in?"

"Sure."

Why was she so mad at me? Arguably she was the one more at fault here. We walked into the living room and, as if I had just killed and eaten his little doggie family, the Devil growled and showed his teeth at me. Allison and I sat on opposite sides of her couch that suddenly seemed absurdly long, like the long dinner table at Bruce Wayne's house where he had dinner with Vicki Vale. I couldn't say that we sat in silence for any period of time because her stupid dog's stare and growl was distracting. Allison was the first to speak. "So is she the reason that you haven't talked to me for the past week?"

Is he the reason that you didn't want to marry me? "Actually, no. I haven't talked to you because I've been upset about you not wanting to marry me. That hurt pretty bad you know."

"So how long before you found her?"

"She found me the next night."

"Wonderful timing, wouldn't you say?"

"Yes, well, I was vulnerable, hurt and lonely and she happens to be a nice girl."

"Have you slept with her yet?" That's got to be the most asked question in these scenarios I'd imagine.

"Yes."

She started crying. I gave her a moment to come around and she continued her interrogation. "Did she tell you that we were friends?"

"Actually, no. I happened to figure that out for myself. Trust me I was pretty angry that she didn't tell me, but clearly I can understand why she wasn't planning on it anytime soon."

It seemed clear that this was all she had thought of to ask me, so it was time for my opening statements. "How's everything with...Sascha, right?"

"Don't make this about me."

"Who else is it about? You know I always had a suspicion that you had a specific reason that you said no, but I never thought it would be another guy."

"What do you mean?"

"How did you actually meet him, and more importantly, when?"

She seemed stunned. I can't believe that she thought Nicole wouldn't tell me something like that after all of this bullshit. "I heard you'd been seeing him for a while, right?"

"I can't believe she told you."

"Well, we are dating now and we're trying to build a relationship based on some semblance of trust."

She looked as though she had just been punched in the stomach, unable to speak with no breath in her lungs. As she recovered, I decided to continue. "You know, I actually had some reservations about ending things with you. Nicole could tell you about it if you ever felt like talking to her again." I went on, "I still loved you very much and hoped that you'd come around and realize how much you needed me too if I wasn't around for a little while. As it turns out you were probably better off without me, right?" No one in their right mind would ever respond to that question, even though everyone involved always knew the right answer. "So how long have you been seeing him?"

Her gaze dropped from my eyes to the floor in shame. "About 3 months."

"He's why you said no, right? He's the reason that you didn't want to marry me."

"Josh, I was just confused about everything."

"And yet you're mad at me for meeting Nicole." The moment I said it I knew I shouldn't have. Of course it was the truth, but she would never allow the fault to be pinned squarely on her. We transformed from a sad, broken couple into another bitter battle.

"Of course I'm fucking mad. She's one of my best friends and you were my boyfriend!" she screamed while Satan barked as her backup yes man.

"Even though you'd been cheating on me for the last 3 months? I fail to see how I'm the bad guy here. If you had just said yes to me, then none of this would have happened." My voice was never raised. I aimed to be the calm, rational one.

"So you're blaming me?"

"Of course I'm blaming you. Who else's fault would it be?"

"You're unbelievable."

"Thanks, I hear that a lot."

It was getting dumb. Nothing can ever be resolved when people are angry. I decided to get straight to the point.

"Look. I didn't come here to fight. I wanted to hear from you that you were in fact with Sascha while we were together, to answer any questions that you may have had about my relationship with Nicole, and to get my ring back."

"Your ring?"

"Yes, if you're not going to marry me I'd like it back."

"You gave it to me."

I looked at her puzzled for a moment. "It's an engagement ring. You didn't agree to the terms of the arrangement and so I'd like it back please."

"I really don't think I should have to give it back after all of this."

"All of what? You said no to me, and what's more, you cheated on me for three months prior to me even buying the thing—which I might add cost me a lot of money that I really need right now after losing my job."

Her eyebrows squinched together and I realized that she had no idea that I had been let go from Starbucks.

"Yeah, I was fired. I really need it back so that I can return it and maybe eat some food and pay rent."

"I don't think I can give it back to you."

It was now my turn to be angry. "What do you mean you can't give it back to me? I need that ring."

"No."

"What the fuck is wrong with you Allison? Why do you think you deserve it? You're not worth half of what that ring is worth!" As I punctuated that sentence I started to get up from the chair to head to her bedroom and take it back.

"What are you doing?" she screamed.

"I'm getting my goddamn ring back!"

"Josh, stop it, get out of here. Get out of my apartment!"

"Not without my ring."

I threw things around in her room, pushing objects off her dresser top, opening drawers of her desk and nightstand. I couldn't find it. This was stupid. Did she just think that she could keep it? What the hell was wrong with her? The constant drone of Allison's screaming and the evil growl of the Devil dog was a backdrop of sound that would have suited a horror flick. Finally I spotted the small, fuzzy box that contained my unemployment check on her bathroom countertop. Right as I started storming through the bathroom door, the dog ran up behind me and bit my leg. Hard. I didn't quite fall down, but I screamed out in pain. I tried to shake him off, but his grip didn't loosen. I turned around and tried to kick Satan in defense, but the angle that he had my leg it, made it impossible to attack with my feet. I never thought I would have to punch anything in my life, let alone a dog, but I clenched my fist and as hard as I could I punched the beast in the side.

I must have struck some soft spot because he quickly recoiled. With my leg finally free, I reeled it back and kicked him again in the same spot. He teetered on his 3 good legs. "Josh, you sick fuck. Get the fuck out of my house! Now!"

"Not without my ring." I grabbed the little box while the dog was still stunned and nearly knocked Allison over on my way out of her bedroom, and ran out the front door. I kept running all the way back to my apartment, without a stop. I thought that bystanders were probably wondering if I had stolen something because I wasn't in running gear, but the apathetic nature of the general public meant that I'd at least make it home without interference. I wondered why robbers didn't wear black tear-away clothes with running outfits underneath. If you're running down the street in athletic gear, no one questions you, but if you're in civvies, then you're immediately suspected of something.

The whole way home, my heart tapped my ribs harder and harder as I ran further, begging me to stop. My leg throbbed with the amplitude and frequency of a Ramones song. I ran up into my room and collapsed onto my bed. I hadn't run in a long time and my lungs and heart weren't used to all this cardiovascular activity. I opened my hand with the treasure box that I had rightfully stolen and just looked at it for a moment as my body calmed down. I flashed back to the moment that I decided to ask Allison the big question. I remembered the exciting but terrifying feeling in my gut. I remembered Christopher, the salesman who helped me pick out this perfect ring. I remembered the feeling of accomplishment and dedication when I was finally buying it. I remembered planning the proposal, talking to Greg's dad and convincing him to keep the carnival open for one final night. Finally, I remembered the feeling when she didn't say yes.

It was with that feeling that I opened up the box to see it. It took my brain a few seconds to realize what my eyes were reporting to it.... It wasn't there. No ring. I waged war on Satan and I didn't leave with anything to show for it. No signs of victory.

13

I rolled up my jeans, stained with a mix of dried blood and devil slobber, and kicked off my shoes. The bastard had gotten me just below my calf and dug in hard. I debated going back to the doctor, but decided against it at the thought of how much another set of hospital bills would set me back, especially without the goddamn ring to return. At least he didn't get my Achilles. I would have had to end up suing Allison for housing a terrorist and I neither had the time, money nor patience to deal with our judicial system. The bleeding had stopped and deciding that it wasn't worth a trip to the ER, I hobbled over to the bathroom. Now that the adrenaline had left my system, I began to feel the pain of the bite with each step, across the hardwood floor all the way to the tiled bathroom.

I found a nearly empty tube of Neosporin and a few small Band-Aids. Where was I when the rest of this tube of Neosporin was used up, I thought. I couldn't remember using any of it, let alone a whole tube of the stuff. Carefully I covered each tooth-sized gash with a band-aid. It took six small band-aids to do the deepest cuts. The rest of the teeth weren't long enough to break the skin, though they did certainly leave a mark. If they could identify a dog from its teeth like they do with humans, my leg could have been Exhibit A in my trial against the heinous dog.

Not wanting to stew in anger or pain, I quickly called Nicole and asked her if the offer still stood for me to go over that night. "Of course," she said wondering why I even asked. "I'll be here, just come on over." When she asked whether I was OK, I told her that I'd explain everything when I came over.

Even though I was broke and had no prospects of making money, I decided that I wouldn't be able to walk the mile or so over to Nicole's and decided that the five dollar cab ride would be well worth it. Being the tech geek that most in my generation are, I hailed a cab online and got a text message when it arrived two minutes later. Nicole's address came as easily out of my mind as my own would have. It's amazing how quickly we get used to new things, places, and people. It's also amazing how fast you can get places when you take a car. Nicole's apartment was right outside the car door within 3 minutes, after hitting all green lights with a driver that didn't believe in speed limits.

When I buzzed up, she assumed it was me and said, "Well that was fast," as a way of saying hello. "Come on up." Of course she didn't mean it the way I heard it, but to me it sounded like, "Oh great... you're here already." The stairs seemed like an obstacle course to me and I realized why I never considered joining the armed forces.

I would have been the one at the back of the line that everyone cheered and teased from the finish line, all of them having completed the course. "You can do it, maggot! Get your ass over here with the rest of us or everyone has to do 500 pushups and clean the bathrooms with our toothbrushes!" No, thank you, to that.

When I finally knocked on the door, Nicole opened it with a "What took you so long to—Oh my God! What happened?" She helped me the rest of the way into her apartment and over to her sofa where I plopped into the same spot as the night before. For a second I wondered which was worse, the feeling I had last night knowing that Allison had betrayed me long before I had made the mistake of asking her to marry me, or the dog bite still clenching my leg. Ultimately I decided that the feelings from last night weren't gone yet, and so today's pain won over all the negative emotions I had about her and life in general.

Nicole, being amazing, was finishing preparations of dinner for the two of us. She made scallop risotto that smelled unbelievable. She had a bottle of wine ready and a few candles set up to be lit for a romantic mood. "I hope I didn't ruin the evening you had planned," I said, wanting her to know that I had noticed everything she had worked so hard on. "Oh, Josh, I certainly know it's not your fault," she said as I made my way to a chair at the table. Right as I sat down, she placed my plate in front of me. I rarely had scallops and I never imagined that the bubbly, slightly nerdy MIT girl that I met at Our House earlier in the week would be cooking them for me, trying to impress me.

Between each amazing bite, I recounted a small chunk of the ridiculous day I had. I told her everything. I told the story about the little ducks at the duck pond, which made her smile. I told her about how I couldn't find my ring and freaked out. I told her about how I called Allison out about Sascha.

"She hates me now, doesn't she?" Nicole asked.

"Well to be fair, she probably started hating you last night. Nothing I said today changed anything. She just still hates you. She actually tried to make me out to be the bad guy. Even after she admitted that she didn't want to marry me because she was unsure of her and me because of her and Sascha."

"Yeah, well we do that. It's always your fault, you know. Whatever it is."

Eventually I told her about my encounter with Allison and her evil dog.

"She refused to give you the ring back?"

"Yeah."

"What? Why? I don't understand."

"You got me."

"What does she want to do with it? Was she wearing it?"

"No, I think I would have noticed that."

"But it wasn't in the box?"

"No."

"You don't think she would have sold it, do you?"

"Apparently you know her just as well as I do, so you tell me. I doubt it. She doesn't need the money."

"Yeah, you're right."

"Could she have lost it, but she didn't want to tell you?"

"Lost it? How could she have lost it?"

"Well I can imagine that if someone asked me to marry them and I was unsure of what I wanted to do, I would have at least tried it on to see what it looked like. Every girl wants an amazing engagement ring. It's a lot like trying on wedding dresses whether you're getting married or not—you like the thought of it."

I often felt as though I understood a lot about girls that many guys didn't, but I certainly never understood their desire for a wedding. Why was it ingrained in their souls? A giant party for what? You're married when you sign some papers, not when a guy waves a magic wand in a church or in a hotel banquet hall. Why not just have a party like any other party and save the money you'd spend on the wedding for retirement or your kid's college fund or anything else?

"Hmm..." I hadn't thought of her losing it.

"Well couldn't she have told me that she lost it instead of demanding that she keep it?"

"Would it have made a difference?"

She was right. I would have been just as upset if she had lost it. I wouldn't have punched and kicked her dog, but I would have hated her just the same either way.

"No, that doesn't add up for me. I know her pretty well and I didn't think that she was hiding anything from me." Then I realized that she had kept Sascha from me for 3 months and I didn't have a clue. "Well, maybe she could be lying, but I don't think she just lost it."

"So it has to be somewhere else in her apartment, right?"

"It has to be."

"So what are you going to do?"

I reached into my pocket and pulled out the little trinket that would elucidate what I was planning. "You still have a key to her place.... You sneaky bastard."

"In all the hullabaloo today, she never thought to ask for it back. It was probably the last thing on her mind, so here's what I'm thinking...." Nicole was genuinely intrigued in knowing my plan. She leaned forward to hear better, excited, listening intently as if she were at a murder mystery dinner playhouse and she had just figured out whodunit. She didn't take much pleasure in having figured it out first, as she was just glad to be a part of it all.

"I was thinking I'd just walk in, snoop around, with gloves of course, and leave with the ring that's rightfully mine." After all, I still had the receipt to prove it. I wondered who would win if it went to court. Perhaps Judge Judy would rule in my favor because of my quirky charm, but Allison would turn on the fireworks and it's hard to tell a girl she can't have her engagement ring when she's bawling–whether the tears are real or not.

"What about the dog?" she asked, like the kid in the front of the class telling the teacher she didn't have enough homework for the night.

"That's where I'm unsure of what to do. I'm hoping that it's still hurt from today, but if it's not, then I don't really have a plan yet."

"Hmm."

We both sat eating our risotto as if it was some sort of magical potion and we were waiting for the acid trip that would reveal the answers to our questions. Unfortunately life doesn't work that way and magic potions are hard to come by these days. The wine certainly helped. Without realizing, during my detailed descriptions of the day's events, I had drunk two full glasses. Apparently Nicole was a ninja trained in the deft art of shadow wine pouring.

It suddenly occurred to me that our relationship up to that point had revolved around alcohol, which seemed odd to me. From the get go, we met at a bar. The rest of the week was one bizarre occurrence after another that deserved a drink or two after having to deal with the drama. I ate the last bite of risotto and bowed to the chef. "Dinner was unbelievable. Thank you." The sincerity of my praise made her blush a bit as she offered to clear the plates. Instead of doing the dishes right away though, she helped me back over to the sofa and sat down next to me with her head on my shoulder as we had been the night before.

"You know, I could really get used to this." I whispered just loud enough to reach her ears, but no further.

"Me too." Her words had to wrap around her head to reach my ears.

All of a sudden she jumped up. "I have an idea!" she exclaimed. "PETA won't approve of this, but it'll probably work." She bounced over to her desk and opened her top drawer. After rustling a few odds and ends around, she pulled out a small case with a snap at the top.

"What is it?" I asked.

"It's a taser."

"You want me to taser a dog? Can you do that?"

"I don't know, but it'll definitely stop him, right?"

She did have a point. I already punched and kicked the thing, would it really make a difference on my moral permanent record if I tased the son of a bitch? A quick tutorial on the usage of the taser and I was ready to go. Aside from the fact that I was a little wounded myself, I was prepared for my mission. We went over possible locations for the ring. "If I were hiding a ring I wouldn't put it somewhere obvious. It wouldn't be with the rest of my jewelry. But she did take it out of the box...." We both made speculations based on what I could remember about her room and the various containers in it. We drew out a little map of her room with all the possible places notated with symbols.

At the end of our secret meeting, the plan sounded so simple: use my key, taser the dog, find the ring and walk out. Satan would be back to normal by the time Allison came home and she probably wouldn't notice the ring was gone until I had already returned it. After going step by step over the plans and all possible locations for the ring, we lounged back in the sofa and took sips of the last of the wine. "We've had quite the eventful relationship so far, haven't we?" I asked playfully.

"We sure have."

"Are we going a good pace?"

"What do you mean?"

"Well both of us just got out of pretty long relationships. You happen to know the extent of mine. I happen to know the severity of yours. I don't want to rush anything with you. I like you. A lot."

Her face melted into a smiling wax statue of herself.

"I think we're going a good pace. Do you?"

"I just wanted to make sure that you're ok with everything."

"I had to practically beg you to stay over. It took that whole mess with Allison to actually make it happen." We both laughed and I wrapped my arm around her shoulder.

"I just like that I already feel comfortable with you even though there's still so much to learn about you. I don't feel like I have to impress you or anything and so I just have a lot of fun with you. Who would have thought plotting a faux felony against my ex-girlfriend could be so fun, right?"

"And my ex-good friend. I'm becoming less and less caring of her well-being. What a terrible friend I am."

"Whose fault is it?"

"What?"

"Who's the bad guy in all of this?"

"What do you mean?"

"Well, I started seeing you without knowledge of Allison's affair. You started seeing me knowing full well that I was Allison's boyfriend. Allison started dating Sascha 3 months before I asked her to marry me and therefore 3 months before I started seeing you. Arguably, everyone involved is at fault for something."

"Why does there have to be a bad guy?"

"I guess I'm just used to the idea that there is always a bad guy in a story. Blame Walt Disney."

"Hmm. Well, everyone was just doing what was good for them, right?"

"Yeah, I suppose."

"Then one could argue that we're all the bad guys."

"Oh."

"Or we can both just blame Allison and call her the bad guy."

"But then she'll just blame us and call us the bad guy."

"And that is how all wars are justified. Everyone thinks that God is on their side and that they are the ones that deserve to win."

"But then—"

"Let's not worry about who's the bad guy here, ok? I'd rather just enjoy the night with you."

"You're right. But she's the bad guy here, right?"

"Absolutely."

She stretched her neck to kiss me. A few moments in tender embrace and she broke away to start doing the dishes. Her computer was the focus of the room for Act Two of that evening as we both checked out our social pages to see what the word was on the digital street. The Bayside Ramblers had written back to me and liked my review as well. Two out of two is a good start and just like Wally and the Whale they had asked me to possibly review their new album when it came out. This whole reviewing thing was going better than I could have expected so far. The only thing to do now was to go see as many shows as I could, or as many shows as I could afford until I found an actual job.

A few more glasses of wine and the fermented grapes called forth the longing in our bodies, like spirits from another plane. Soon we had re-staged the performance of the night before. Lying there before falling asleep I asked her, "Do you think this is a bad idea?"

"What, us?"

I laughed. "No I'm sorry. My plot for tomorrow. Is it ridiculous?"

"What's ridiculous is her not giving you back the ring. You have an odd sort of right to being wrong on this one. I've known her for a long time and it still just doesn't seem like something that she'd do."

A breath or two. "I know, right? That's what worries me about the whole thing. She's been so out of character for the past few weeks. You think she's ok?"

"I don't think either of us will be able to find out at this point."

"Yeah."

The thick Boston wind whirred and screeched against the windows of her apartment, like fingernails dragged across a chalkboard. Eventually the exhaustion and wine took over my body and I drifted off to sleep. That night I dreamt of Allison. I would rather have dreamt about the angry, drunken carnie ramming his car into the carnival again, than dream of her.

She was sitting quietly at home reading a book, looking rather sullen. She kept switching positions, never finding one that she could sink into and relax. She just couldn't stay still. Her whole afternoon went like that. She had a glass of wine to help her relax, but even that didn't help. Someone came to her door. Of course, it was Sascha, except he didn't look like the tool he was when I met him. He looked like a sophisticated guy. As he walked through the door, she immediately took off her shirt, ran over and jumped on him. It went on and on and on. I knew that I was sleeping but I couldn't wake up and I couldn't control anything. It was as if my mind was forcing me to watch, holding my internal eyelids open.

I woke up to Nicole wiping my forehead and whispering, "Shhh, it's ok. Shhh." I jumped up and landed back down in the same position. "Bad dream?" Nicole asked.

"Terrible." I told her all about it, sparing her the details that no one would really want to hear. After about five minutes I finally started to calm down and started to think about Allison in the dream. I couldn't remember any time when she was as excited to see me as she was seeing Sascha. It was as if Sascha were a drug and she was addicted to him. Restless until she got her fix of someone other than me. It was terrifying.

"I just have to tell you, so that it won't fester inside me. I'm not all that mad, but it does bother me a bit. Forgetting for a moment that you knew that I was dating Allison, you still knew that she was dating Sascha, right?"

"Yes."

"And you didn't tell me, why?"

"That would have given away that I knew her."

"Right."

"I was going to eventually tell you. I just didn't want to be the reason that everything ended. I wanted you guys to work it out as if I weren't there."

"I don't understand that."

"I'm sorry."

"What can you do? Everyone's the bad guy here, right?"

"Yeah, I guess so."

That morning we decided to forego the usual habits of the last few days and we went out for breakfast. My leg felt surprisingly better and I could walk normally again. We made our way to a small café that sat like a fat cat on the edge of the MIT campus. Everyone came to it in spite of the usual long wait, and for good reason. A meal fit for a warrior was what I needed and that's exactly what I got. I hadn't eaten so much in one sitting in years. It wasn't heavy, though. I ate and ate and just felt my body absorbing everything that it could to prepare me for what lay ahead.

We went over the plans and I made sure I had all my tools. Nicole paid the tab and then kissed me for good luck before waving goodbye and walking briskly to her class. Fear crawled up my legs, grabbing at the top of my pants to hoist itself up. Then it grabbed my spine like a shaky ladder and climbed higher up to my neck. I got a cab to quickly take me across the bridge as walking across it would still have been tricky. I got out at the top of Newbury because the cabbie didn't understand my directions, so and I decided that a coffee would do me good. I needed that extra jolt to get the job done right.

I went back into Starbucks by 'the Nasty' and got myself a large coffee. Even though I worked there, I still refuse to say tall, grande and venti. Just make it small, medium or large. Please. A seat was open by the window and I decided that a moment to prepare would be nice. People watching was a sport in this city and I was one of the team captains. One of the best. A couple caught my attention as they broke stride and pulled their hands apart right across the street. The girl was yelling at the guy and he looked horrified. Normally if someone is yelling at you like that, you know what you did. He seemed completely clueless.

Maybe he was just acting like he didn't know, but I didn't think so. The poor guy was getting berated by what seemed to be his girl, right in the middle of a busy pedestrian highway. They blocked foot traffic, and if people had horns built-in, there would have been many of them honking at the two. She slowly made the transition from anger to tears. I had never seen a girl yell like that without eventually ending up dripping in tears. I was so caught up in my own life that I forgot other people out there were likely having their own dramas, like I was having the last few days. Maybe names and events were changed, but enough was the same to make any life a movie "based on a true story".

I had more sympathy for both of them than I would have, eight days ago. I probably would have blamed him for being the one to do something wrong, when really she was probably trying to blame him to hide what she had done. We're an amazing species, I thought, as I checked my pockets for the taser and the keys to Allison's apartment. Tossing the empty coffee cup into the trash, I walked out the door and imagined that I was walking in slow motion like in a Wes Anderson movie. The hero's moment of slow motion. Mine came as I approached the apartment building soon to be six thousand dollars less valuable.

The key worked, which was a good start. It felt oddly sensual, easing softly into the keyhole. I was trying to be gentle so as not to stir the beast until I was good and ready. (I had envisioned a scenario, while searching for the right key, where Allison somehow had time to change the locks before I got there and I had to climb up some ivy and break a window.) I simply wanted what was mine, not to actually break and enter. Prison seemed repugnant like one of those really soft smelly French cheeses that I did not ever feel like tasting; not even accompanied by the best wine.

The door opened quietly, surprisingly silent for an old wooden door. There was just a whisper as the draft guard slid against the hardwood floors. With my first step into her apartment I felt like I was about to step onto the moon. I felt as though I had never been there before. I had been alone in her place many times, but I had never walked into her place when she wasn't there, and I hoped it would be the last time.

With the second step, I was in. The door closed behind me just as quietly as it had opened—Stage 1 of this game had been cleared with great marks. Stage 2 started as I noticed the Devil sleeping in the corner of the living room. I wondered what Satan dreams about. Attacking humans? Kid-face sandwiches? Biting innocent boyfriends? I was sure I saw him licking his lips as he growled in his sleep. I stepped as quietly as I could walking toward her bedroom one step at a time, trying to remember where the creaks in the wood were. I used the wood grain lines and spots like constellations to find my way through the wooden sea. Peering over my shoulder as I entered the doorway to the bedroom, I checked the status of The Evil One. By the hand of Zeus he was still sleeping.

The snooping began. The first place I looked was in her drawers where I started last time. This time I'd be more methodical and thorough. Top drawer, bottom drawer. Nothing. Next we had thought to go to the jewelry box—though obvious, Allison wasn't a very creative one. Her jewelry had no news of my ring, though I did catch a few things that I'd never seen before. Fucking Sascha. I wondered how long ago she was given those as gifts, but any conclusion I might have reached would not have been good news, so I stopped thinking of it altogether. There was no time for anger here.

I double-checked the top of her desk, which was rather cluttered. Nothing. Nightstand. Nothing. Even the bathroom. Nothing. I was getting frustrated. Where else could it be? In my frustration I stepped on a spot of the floor that I knew was going to give me away. The part of my mind that was supposed to be looking out for the floor had teamed up with the rest of me in brainstorming and neglected its duties. Immediately I heard that all-too-familiar sound. Satan had risen prematurely from his sleep, and he was pissed.

I unsnapped the taser from its case and got ready for him. I clicked it on to make sure that it worked as he started his short run towards me. The blue glow from the taser didn't halt his steps at all, and though I tried to stop him he jumped so high that his head was eye level with me. My arm swung out with my thumb pressing the trigger and it struck him right in the side. A puppyish squeal was all that was left of his energy as his body fell hard and limp onto the ground. I was so astonished that I couldn't move. It took a moment for me to remember what I was there to do. Cover blown, I ran full speed into the bathroom and rummaged through the drawers and cabinets like in a police raid. I tried not to be too fast for fear of missing something, but I had no idea how long the shock would keep him out and wasn't going to be around long enough to find out.

It wasn't there. I ran into the kitchen and looked through the pots and pans, I looked by the TV, I looked on the shelves of the small entertainment center. Nothing. The Demon was stirring and still I had nothing. The moment I heard the barking of the discombobulated dog coming back to life, I was suddenly enraged. I grabbed the taser from my pocket and started walking over to him ready to stun him again for more time. He was trying to convince his legs to stand as I pulled the trigger on the taser and slammed it once again into his side. Only that time, it didn't turn on. "You have got to be kidding me!" I yelled at the dog. I pulled the trigger again. Nothing. Repeatedly I smacked it onto the ground hoping that might shake some sense back into the thing. This was no time for the key member of the strike force to go down.

It looked as if he understood what was happening. He had to have remembered the device that caused him so much pain, despite his immense stupidity. It was simple survival. He looked at me, then at the taser, then back again. The spark of his evil erupted into fire all around him, and the heat struck an intense fear in me down to my intestines. For the first time in our battles together, he knew that he had the upper hand. I could see it in his eyes. He was going to hurt me. Bad. The insurgents finally had a chance to take down the powers that had oppressed them for so long.

In a desperate move, I ordered my foot to strike the dog. I never thought I'd be a puppy kicker, but again I had never met Satan either. Things change so fast. Apparently I wasn't fast enough for the sudden rush of power that the Devil had found. He dodged my foot and growled with the zeal of a lion protecting his offspring. As I slowly marched my way backwards towards the door, he followed me step for step. I thought that maybe if I just left, he'd leave me alone, content with his victory. As I turned to reach for the door, he leapt at me with jowls wide open ready to embrace my flesh in a murderous hug.

Somehow I was quick enough to just dodge teeth, but his body rammed into me hard enough to knock me over. We fell like angry lovers to the floor as he slobbered all over me. With a sudden rush of strength I threw him off of me and turned over to make my escape. As I stood up to slam the door behind me cueing this awful scene to wrap, the beast was right behind me in the doorway. That was it. I had to call retreat. There was nothing else I could do. So I started to run.

That's where this whole story started. It was soon thereafter that we battled in the street and I retrieved the ring, covered in evil slobber, from Satan's dirty mouth. I met the wonderful Darla and Herbert and eventually made my way back to Allison's to return the broken and defeated warrior. I walked home that night to my own apartment instead of Nicole's. We had planned for me to rendezvous back with her that night, but I just needed some time to myself. The whole thing was just too much to take in. I called her as I walked home and told her briefly what happened, without any exciting details, telling her that I'd fill her in later on the rest. The key point was that overall it was a success. I had the ring.

At home, I kicked off my shoes, poured myself some whiskey and went into the bathroom. First thing was first. I had to clean the gunk off the ring. If I was going to return it, I needed to make it look like it hadn't been wrapped around a rottweiler's tooth for the past who-knows-how-many-days. I wondered how it ended up in his mouth, let alone securely wrapped around a tooth. I had a hard time imagining the scenario. I made a mental note to ask Allison, years down the line if we became friends again. I wondered if that's why she was so adamant about not giving it back. Had she though that she lost it? A string to a light bulb just above my head was pulled on and I laughed out loud.

She thought she lost it. It made so much sense. She would have probably given it back readily, but she didn't want to admit that she lost it and so she refused to give it back. That had to be it. As I tucked that little secret into my pocket to possibly use at a later date, the ring was just about clean. I held it up toward the light and it sparkled like a newborn star. "You little son of a bitch." I scolded the twinkling ring. "You have changed my life forever." Engagement rings were supposed to do that to the person giving it and to the girl they give it to. In my case, though, it showed me a girl more suited for me and got me away from a girl that I would have been miserable with, especially given her long-standing affair with a euro-trash prick named Sascha.

14

The next morning I felt as if I had slept on a bed of angel wings. Sure it was unbelievably comfortable, but I had a small pang of guilt knowing that a few angels probably had to die or at least become human to make my good night possible. I rolled off the soft warmth of heaven and onto the chilly floor of reality. The gates of my bathroom welcomed me and I cranked on the shower. I didn't shampoo or soap for the first 5 minutes. I hardly moved at all. I just stood there enraptured by the feeling that I was finally free. I was free from any ties with Allison. I no longer felt like

I owed her anything or that she owed me anything in return. I was free of my worry about my temporary unemployment. I knew I was okay for a while and that I'd find something, even if it was something stupid, until I finally found what was right for me. I was free of any fear of the devil dog. I was his greatest enemy, but I had helped him and he had helped me in an offbeat kind of way. Mostly, I was free of any guilt of meeting Nicole. Knowing someone's story helps you understand who they are and I was finally starting to understand Allison and what she needed. I realized that I wasn't what she needed. And I was okay with that.

It all started to make sense that day as I rode the "T" downtown to Freedman Jewelers. As I rode past each stop, I watched everyone waiting for their own train. People going about their lives, with all their worries and secrets stapled to their shirts, except that they were written in a language that only the person wearing it could understand. They passed each other, occasionally exchanging a passing glance or wave—but ultimately they each lived in their own world. I wondered what life would be like if people could read each other's internal languages and know everyone else's stories. No more doubt—just truth, what was actually happening, hanging out around our necks for everyone to see. The idea was so farfetched that I could only hold onto it for a few seconds, and then it was gone.

By the time I stopped at Government Center and got off the train, it all went away. Life's canvas was suddenly covered in a spill of Gesso, putting everything back to a sterile blank white. Everyone just looked like they always did. Christopher looked the way he did when I bought the ring—just a guy doing his job, trying to make a living. When I told him the abridged version of my past few days, his eyes stayed wide open during the whole story. I couldn't tell if he was excited to hear such a tale or frightened by the whole ordeal. After apologies and suggestions that I keep the ring for later, they courteously refunded my six grand and reminded me to come back to them when the time was right. I happily agreed.

I called Nicole before returning to Back Bay and asked if she wanted to hang out later. We chatted for a moment about what we should do, but ultimately I persuaded her that we should stay in for the night and I'd tell her all about the trials of the day. Of course, she was fine with that and suggested that she'd make a fancy dinner. Of course, I was fine with that.

Allison was the next and final call for the day. I knew that she had the day off and I asked her if we could meet somewhere and talk. There was no way that I wanted to be in the same room as Satan—we both needed time apart. We agreed to meet on Newbury at Tealuxe, a little tea shop that was the only place you could order tea and crumpets. The place was always somehow filled with people who had been fighting for days. Some for years. It was a modern, secular Reconciliation booth. A place of understanding and peace. No wars were fought there, only after an armistice was declared could two people enter its doors.

I was already seated when she arrived. We hugged cordially and after hanging her coat up, she sat down across from me. There was an unusual sense of commonality between us. We both felt the same things in different ways and we both finally noticed it. After the first cup of tea, we started to open up a little. I asked her to tell me about how she met Sascha, and after giving me a look that said "Are you sure?" she realized that I was actually interested. So she began. They had met way back in college, remaining friends throughout the years. He had always had a crush on her—more than a crush, really, he had been in love with her. She said that he asked her out every once-in-a-while, never relenting, even after so many rejections.

He never did let go. Years later he was still asking her out with the same zeal as when they had first met. I never would have kept that up, I thought, as she continued. One night he asked her to go out to dinner with him—as friends, of course. She hesitantly agreed and he took her to the Top of the Hub, a swanky restaurant at the top of the Prudential Center, the second tallest building in the city.

Everything was going fine as a friendly date, until he got down on one knee, and asked her to marry him. Her answer was, of course, no.

But it sowed the seeds of doubt. It also helped that he had become quite successful in his business and I, of course, was doing no such thing. That was 3 months prior to my proposal. They started hanging out more and more after that, still as 'friends.' Except now, instead of asking her out, he was periodically asking her to marry him. You had to give the guy kudos on his persistence if you could get past the slicked back, greasy hair. She turned down all of his proposals as a good girlfriend would until one night her curiosity led her astray. She let him kiss her. She admitted that it was unusual and different and that she was so used to me that it didn't seem right. She let it continue and eventually, they started dating.

I was somehow completely oblivious to all of this, though none of it surprised me anymore. I just listened, genuinely interested in her story. For weeks leading up to my proposal, she went out with him occasionally on the nights that I decided to stay at home. As I sat at my computer, listening to music, or playing video games, she was out with him having the time of her life. By the time I got around to asking her to marry me, she had been dating Sascha for months and was so confused about what she wanted out of life that she couldn't accept my proposal.

Two men wanted to marry her. One was a twenty something deadbeat wannabe writer who worked at Starbucks. The other was a twenty something entrepreneur with a blossoming international business. One offered her a ring worth six grand, the other offered her a ring worth twenty. On paper there was an obvious choice, but in her heart there was love. She loved me, she explained, but she was a woman that needed security as well as love. It would have been nice to live in a fairy tale, she said, but in the real world she had to make the best decision that she could for her future. It turns out that love is only true in film and song. In real life it's just statistics.

When it was my turn, I told my story simply, without too many bells and whistles. Just the truth as it would have been shown to the world in that alternate universe where everyone's inner life was transparent. I told her about how I met Nicole. How she unabashedly broke me free and made me dance to ridiculous 80s classics. I told her about how she disappeared that night without any reason or word. I told her about how I got fired from Starbucks and how triumphant I felt as I walked out those doors. I told her how I found Nicole the next day, most likely because of a dream I had. I told her about how Nicole tricked me into going to a swing club and how I passed out from exhaustion. I told her about our first kiss there on the bridge, and how I went home every night because I didn't want to hurt her. I told her about how I figured out that they knew each other and what that meant for me.

Then we both took turns talking about what happened after we saw each other out on dates with other people at the Square. I felt so comfortable there at that table with her, drinking tea and eating crumpets with jam, that I almost told her about the ring. She never said anything and so I had to assume that my guess was correct. She thought she lost it and she was glad that I hadn't brought it up, not knowing that I had not only retrieved it, but had returned it that very day. The check came and we split it down the middle. "I'm glad we got together, Josh. You have no idea how worried I was when you saw me with Sascha. My anger was really contorted fear."

"I know. I was pretty scared myself."

We smiled awkwardly at each other before embracing each other in a hug that lasted a few ticks longer than a friendly hug would. Pulling back, she smiled her natural smile that I had seen a million times before but never fully appreciated, and never would have the chance to again. And that was ok.